DANGER

NEXT DOOR

RED STONE SECURITY SERIES

Katie Reus

Cover art: Jaycee of Sweet 'N Spicy Designs
Author website: http://www.katiereus.com

Danger Next Door/Katie Reus. -- 1st ed.
ISBN-13: 978-1497439955
ISBN-10: 1497439957

eISBN: 9780988617155

For my sister.

Praise for the novels of Katie Reus

"Wow! This powerful, passionate hero sizzles with sheer deliciousness. I loved every sexy twist of this fun & exhilarating tale. Katie Reus delivers!" —Carolyn Crane, RITA award winning author

"Has all the right ingredients: a hot couple, evil villains, and a killer action-filled plot. . . . [The] Moon Shifter series is what I call Grade-A entertainment!" —Joyfully Reviewed

"I could not put this book down. . . . Let me be clear that I am not saying that this was a good book *for* a paranormal genre; it was an excellent romance read, *period.*" —All About Romance

"Reus strikes just the right balance of steamy sexual tension and nail-biting action....This romantic thriller reliably hits every note that fans of the genre will expect." —*Publishers Weekly*

"Prepare yourself for the start of a great new series! . . . I'm excited about reading more about this great group of characters." —Fresh Fiction

"Nonstop action, a solid plot, good pacing and riveting suspense..." —*RT Book Reviews (4.5 Stars)*

"Katie Reus pulls the reader into a story line of second chances, betrayal, and the truth about forgotten lives and hidden pasts." —The Reading Café

G rant pressed his back against the outside wall of the turquoise and white two-story home he and a team of Miami PD officers were about to storm. On the surface the place fit in perfectly into the upper middle class neighborhood. On the inside, however, it was a fully functioning cocaine lab.

He shifted down a few inches, nearing the corner of the wall. They'd received three solid tips—one from one of Grant's CIs—and had gotten word the lucrative business would be moving in two days. So, they'd had to move fast. As a detective Grant usually didn't participate in stings like this anymore, but he'd been on SWAT for two years and he still missed the rush. Plus the current SWAT team was outside the First Bank of Miami in a twelve hour stand-off with armed robbers so the department was incredibly short-staffed.

They didn't have time to waste. Not when these assholes would be setting up shop again and the department had no clue where.

Dressed in black from head to toe, wearing his standard issue Kevlar vest and tactical gear he hadn't worn in years, he was ready to go. They all were. Holding his M-

4 in a practiced grip, adrenaline pumped through him at lightning speeds.

"On the count of three, we go in. Everyone confirm." The voice of their team leader, Ramirez, sounded in his ear.

There were four total members of the breach team at the front door and four—including Grant—in the back. Any more than eight to do the actual sweep would be too much.

After they all confirmed, Grant waited for the countdown. They also had men covering the windows outside and still others would remain at the front and back doors in case anyone tried to escape. Since Grant had more experience and he had a personal reason for wanting to bring this house down, he was going in the backdoor with three other guys. The windows were all covered with thick, dark blackout curtains so they couldn't see in but thanks to one of the tips they had a pretty good idea what the layout looked like.

When Ramirez hit three everyone moved like a deadly choreographed force. Grant rounded the corner and raced for the back door, his three teammates behind him. Ramirez shouted "Police!" from the front and Grant kicked in the backdoor with a solid strike of his heel.

Weapon raised, he swept in. Three women wearing nothing but underwear—so they couldn't steal the product—all screamed and threw their hands in the air. They were just workers and wouldn't fight back. Not a surprise. If anything they'd probably cut a deal on whoever their boss was.

"On the floor and keep your hands above your head!" Donaldson, one of the guys with him shouted.

As the women complied, Grant keyed his radio, letting everyone know he was moving through the house. He also motioned with his hands for the other two men to fan out as he passed through one of the entryways. The guys coming in from the front needed to be aware of all their movements.

He quickly passed through the kitchen into a dining room and nearly froze at the sight in front of him. A boy with dark curly, almost shaggy hair about six years old sat at a flimsy square folding table with a crayon in his hand and construction paper in front of him. His brown eyes were wide and he was shaking as he stared at Grant.

Pissed that someone had their kid here, Grant held a finger to his mouth and scanned the room, careful to keep his weapon pointed away from the kid. He knew he looked scary as hell dressed in all his tactical gear and carrying a big weapon, but there was nothing he could do about it. No one had even hinted that a child might be here so they weren't prepared with a social worker once this mess was over. Whoever had brought their kid to this fucking house shouldn't have been allowed to procreate.

Seeing slight movement behind one of the dark curtains, Grant took a few steps in that direction. Afraid whoever was behind it might try to use the kid as a hostage or just plain hurt the boy, Grant picked up his pace.

As he did, the kid shook his head, eyes widening in panic. "No!"

Confused for a second, Grant frowned until he heard the soft clicking sound. Shit, shit, *shit*! That sound was unfortunately familiar. He'd trained enough to know exactly what to look for.

Fuckers in these drug houses often set up simple traps. They'd take a rectangular can of black powder with a screw on cap, drill out a hole and place a 209 shotgun primer in it. Once they'd fixed it with a firing pin all they needed was a tripwire.

And he'd just tripped it.

He'd been so focused on the kid he hadn't paid attention to anything else, especially possible booby traps. Never in his life had he made a mistake like this. It was as if everything around him moved into slow motion at that low sound. Above him he could hear part of the team sweeping the rooms, looking for more guys. He also heard the sound of the window breaking—likely whoever was behind that curtain trying to escape.

But all he could actually concentrate on was the boy and getting him out of the blast zone. Adrenaline shot through Grant with the intensity of a fifty cal. He acted purely on instinct. Slinging the rifle over his shoulder he dove at the kid, using his body as a shield.

A split second later an explosion ripped through the air. Heat tore at his back as he tackled the boy, their bodies skidding across the hardwood floor as the table crumpled under Grant's weight. Curling around the kid, he cried out in agony as the flames licked over him, searing through flesh and muscle. Then blackness engulfed him.

CHAPTER ONE

6 Months later

Grant opened his eyes at the sound of his cell phone buzzing across the nightstand. The insistent hum was going to drive him insane. Grabbing it, he looked at the caller ID then shoved the phone under his pillow.

It was Porter. Again.

He loved his oldest brother—okay, his whole family, but he wished they'd leave him the hell alone. If he decided to take the job at Red Stone Security and work with both his brothers and father he'd do it when he was damn well good and ready.

And not a minute sooner.

He rolled onto his side, ignoring the stiffness in his shoulders. Right now he was just trying to keep it together. After leaving the Miami Police Department he felt lost for the first time in his life. Not something he was used to. Right out of high school he'd joined the Marines just like his big brother had done. Four years later after an honorable discharge he'd joined the Miami PD. His first two years as a rookie he'd gone to night school while working as a patrolman. When he'd made

SWAT he'd spent the next two years finishing up with his Bachelor's degree in Criminal Justice. And for the last two he'd been working as a detective and he loved it.

Well, *had* loved it.

Now he was on temporary disability and trying to figure out what he was doing with his life. Half a year ago things had been so clear. He'd had his entire life mapped out. Now, not so much.

Forcing himself to get out of bed and to stop the fucking pity party he was about to have, he took a quick shower and didn't bother looking in the mirror before or after. Seeing his scars only reminded him of what a deformed monster he was. No thanks. He thought about it enough and didn't need the visual aids.

Making his way to the kitchen he avoided glancing at picture frames dotting his hallway walls or anywhere else. They were all filled with pictures of his happy smiling family. His brother Porter and fiancé Lizzy. Or his brother Harrison and gorgeous wife Mara. Or his brothers, father and Grant, *before* the accident.

When he'd been a normal guy. Not Hollywood handsome, but good looking enough to get laid on a regular basis. Now...fuck, he hated the bitterness welling up inside him.

He was alive and had a great family. He'd get over it. Just not today. As he started making a pot of coffee he glanced out his kitchen window and into his neighbor's window and froze.

He had the perfect view of his new neighbor. She was beautiful. Scratch that. The word didn't even come close to describing her. There'd been moving guys in and out of the two-story house all day yesterday but he'd had no clue who was actually moving in. Holy shit, if *that* was her he'd probably scare the hell out of her the first time she saw him. Gorgeous women like her did not associate with someone like him. It would only make her self-conscious or worse—pity him.

But she wasn't even aware of his presence so he could drink in his fill right now. Even if he did feel a little like a peeping Tom.

She didn't seem very tall, though it was hard to measure. Her dark wavy hair cascaded down over her shoulders, reaching just below her breasts. Very full breasts. Definitely enough to fill his palms. And the tight tank top she was wearing left very little to the imagination. It was obvious she'd just woken up as she rubbed a hand over her face and reached for the coffee pot.

Look away, he ordered himself.

But he was rooted to the spot. There was a lot of natural light shining into her kitchen from the windows at the back of her house. He couldn't see the other windows from his angle, but he'd been inside the house before his former elderly neighbors moved out, and it was bathing her like she was some sort of goddess.

Yawning, she stretched her arms over her head and showed off a nice expanse of toned, tanned belly and—yep, he was walking away now.

Before he really did turn into some sort of pervert. Time to work out and do his leg exercises and *not* think about the beauty next door. He'd never walk completely normally again but damned if he wouldn't get close. After completely blowing his knee out when he'd tackled that kid, he'd since had two surgeries. Now there was nothing more doctors could do. He had pins in his knee and he just had to work on getting used to using all his muscles again. Spending time gawking at his neighbor wasn't going to do him any good.

A couple hours later he'd worked out his upper body and had spent some serious time on the treadmill. Sure he wasn't jogging, but he wasn't slowly walking anymore either. Knowing when he'd pushed himself to the limit he changed into his bathing suit and found relief as he descended the steps to his swimming pool.

Immediately the pressure on his leg eased, giving him that weightless relief. Floating on his back, he savored the way his muscles pulled and stretched as he slowly did the backstroke. It wasn't quite noon yet, but the sun was high and bright in a cloudless sky. Since it was April there was a cool breeze but spring in Florida was more like early summer than anything. As he glided through the water he paused at the sound of shouting.

Lifting his head out of the pool, his feet touched the cement in the shallow end. A raised male voice came from the direction of next door. Then the sound of a distressed female voice—with a healthy dose of panic.

Hell no.

Not caring enough to stop and cover up he got out of the water. The voices grew even louder. Cursing his limp, he yanked open the door to his privacy fence, then tried his neighbor's. It easily swung open.

For a moment Grant saw red at the scene in front of him. A tall, lean dark-haired man with an olive complexion had his hands wrapped around the upper arms of the woman he'd seen this morning through the window. The woman was struggling against him, her hand on the middle of the man's chest. The bastard only tightened his grip.

"What the fuck are you doing?" Grant boomed, his voice just a notch short of shouting.

The two people froze. When the man looked over his shoulder at Grant his hands immediately dropped, though his expression was hostile. "Who are you?"

"I live next door," he said, lowering his voice this time. "And you didn't answer me."

Relief flicked in the woman's green eyes as she took a not-so-subtle step back from the man, rubbing her upper arms where the imprint of the man's fingers stood out on her smooth skin.

"This is a private matter," the man said, his dark eyes flashing with annoyance.

Grant ignored him as he focused on the clearly frightened gorgeous woman. "Is this man your boyfriend or family member?" Not that Grant really cared because this asshole was leaving no matter what. He just wanted to know what type of situation he was dealing with.

The woman snorted, taking him by surprise. "No. And he was just leaving."

The man swiveled back to her and took a step forward. "Damn it—"

Grant had moved across the few yards before he'd realized it. The man was about an inch taller than him, putting him at six foot three. But he was lean and a little lanky and even with Grant's bad leg he had no doubt he could flatten him. Hand to hand combat was his specialty and something told him that a guy who didn't have a problem roughing up a woman would be a complete pussy up against a man.

Something about Grant's expression must have conveyed he was ready to take him down because the guy lifted his hands and took a small step back, nearly tripping over his feet. "This was just a misunderstanding."

"The lady told you to leave." There was an edge to Grant's voice.

The man shot an angry look at the woman but hurried toward the gate. Once he reached it he said, "This isn't over," as he practically sprinted away.

Staying where he was, Grant ran his gaze over the woman. He tried to keep it clinical, but it was difficult. Petite but curvy, the brunette had her arms wrapped tightly around herself. Now that he was seeing her up close he realized she likely had Mediterranean heritage. Her skin was a smooth, olive complexion similar to the man who'd just left. But her face was incredibly pale, almost ashen.

Not wanting to scare her, he stayed immobile even though something deep inside him told him to gather her in his arms and comfort her. Yeah, he was sure that would go over real well.

Clearing his throat, he said, "I'm Grant Caldwell. I live next door. Are you okay?"

She opened her mouth, those full lips parting—making him think thoughts he had no business thinking—but just as quickly she shut it as she shook her head. That's when he realized her entire body was shaking.

Shit.

"Did he hurt you?" he growled, ready to go after the guy.

She shook her head again.

As a detective—*former* detective—he'd dealt with plenty of victims before. Not that he was even certain she was one, but he didn't like seeing any female in distress.

"Why don't you have a seat?" He motioned to one of the cushioned patio chairs underneath the porch overhang.

Nodding, she collapsed onto one of them. Aware that he was dripping wet, but not wanting to hover and freak her out further, he sat on the edge of the one next to her. "Do I need to call someone or—"

"No. God, no. Sorry, I'm not normally so...at a loss for words. That was Paulos and long, annoying story short, he's a giant ass. He's the son of my parents' friends, the Balis's and...you so don't need to hear my entire life story." She let out a long breath as she focused those emerald green eyes on him. "I promise to be a drama-free neighbor. I know this is an awful first impression." She smiled self-deprecatingly and he sucked in a quiet breath.

The woman should *not* be allowed to smile. It made her...stunning. In his foggy brain he groped for words, realizing he needed to respond. "What just happened was clearly not your fault. I'm with—was with the Miami PD and it looked like that guy was manhandling you."

"I know. I'm not even going to deny it, but I can't deal with him right now and I don't want to make an issue of it. He surprised me and it won't happen again and...God, I haven't even introduced myself. I'm Belle

Manikas. Thanks for coming to my rescue even though I have a feeling that right now you're trying to think of a polite way to get the hell out of here and away from the crazy neighbor."

Grant couldn't help it. A bark of laughter escaped as she rambled. He could listen to this woman talk all day. "No, I'm not." He glanced over his shoulder to the gate, thinking about the guy Paulos.

"He won't be back. Not today anyway. Trust me," she said quietly.

He wanted to grill her, but knew this wasn't the time or place. Whoever that guy was wouldn't be bothering her again if Grant had anything to say about it. But he needed to get more info from her and he had to be subtle about it. "Listen, I was about to turn on the grill and cook some burgers in the backyard for an early lunch. Want to meet me in about twenty minutes?" Not wanting to leave her alone but not wanting to sit around with his scarred body visible for much longer, Grant tossed the invitation out there.

The second the words were out he wanted to take them back. The majority of his scars were on his back but his left arm was completely covered too. Not to mention his neck and part of his face. It wasn't the same angry red puckered markings from even two months ago, but the fading marks were very visible and not going away. Oddly enough she didn't even seem to notice.

Of course he knew that she did, but she wasn't staring at them. Probably because she was still in a state of shock or something.

What the hell was he thinking? He hadn't had much social contact with anyone in the last six months and considering his constant dark mood he wasn't fit for decent company. Unfortunately the thought of *not* getting to know this woman was almost depressing.

Smiling, she nodded. "Sure. Maybe I can prove to you I'm not going to be your crazy neighbor. Want me to bring anything over?"

Not trusting himself to say anything more, he shook his head, stood and backed toward the fence. He kept his body turned from her, not wanting to give her the full view and scare the hell out of her. As soon as he shut the fence door behind himself, he frowned at his stupidity. What the hell was he doing?

* * *

Belle smoothed a hand over her denim skirt with shaking hands before knocking on her neighbor's door. God, he probably thought she was a lunatic. Part of her worried that Grant had asked her over out of politeness and was now regretting the invite.

When the door opened a second later she couldn't help but smile for her sexy, brooding, scarred neighbor.

He was wearing a long-sleeved T-shirt which was surprising given the warmer weather. Did he have it on to hide the scars she'd seen on his left arm earlier? She didn't care about stuff like that—she had a scar of her own—but maybe it bothered him. Though with those startling blue, almost indigo eyes, it was hard to look anywhere but into those depths. When he'd scared Paulos off earlier she'd been mesmerized by Grant's eyes. Well, that and his *clear* strength. The man was built like a linebacker and in incredibly good shape. It was hard to miss that kind of raw power.

After the way he'd come to her rescue, but kept an obvious distance so he wouldn't scare her, she knew he was safe. It felt weird to link that word with such a huge man but deep in her gut she sensed it. Considering that her family was so big, loud and annoyingly overprotective she'd finally moved out just to get some freaking peace and quiet, she hadn't thought she'd want to spend time with anyone but herself. But grilling out with a neighbor was normal. Doing that with thirty-one of your first freaking cousins on a regular basis—not so much. And God knew she craved some normalcy in her life.

Grant gave her a heated look that took her off guard for a moment before he glanced down at the package in her hand. Eyes narrowing, he paused. "What is that?"

"Uh, I didn't want to come over empty-handed and thought maybe we could pop this in the oven or something." Belle didn't cook well—much to her mother's horror—so she'd brought over a package of premade cookie dough. Also something that could quite possibly give her mother a heart attack. But it was all she'd had in her refrigerator other than baking soda and eggs.

Her neighbor's lips quirked up and he laughed, a deep bold sound. It was the second time he'd done it since they'd met and she had to admit that she loved the sound. It did something strange to her insides, making her...aware of how very male Grant was.

"Thanks." He took the package, still chuckling under his breath as he led her into his foyer.

She noticed he kept the left side of his face turned away from her even when he'd laughed and it bothered her. The fading red marks that covered the side of his face and his ear were definitely noticeable, but it wasn't as bad as he obviously thought it was. She nearly snorted at the thought of this blatantly sexual man trying to hide part of himself from her. God, who didn't have scars whether physical or emotional? Besides, the type of man who rushed over at the sound of a stranger in distress— that was the kind of person she wanted to know.

Belle wanted to tell him to stop but figured it probably wouldn't help her in the 'first impression' department. Once they got to know each other better—well, if they became friendly neighbors—she hoped he'd relax enough around her to stop worrying about it.

Following him down a long hallway she was bombarded with a plethora of pictures. Definitely of Grant and his family. Most of them were with him and two other men who looked similar. His brothers no doubt. A lot of them looked recent and Grant didn't have any scarring, telling her they were fairly new.

Which she could have guessed anyway. She'd noticed that part of his arm still had pinkish angry looking marks while other areas had faded. Since she worked in the hospital she'd seen enough burn victims to understand he'd still be healing for a while.

Her own giant surgical scar in the middle of her chest had faded with time, but the paler skin was still stark against her darker skin. Most of the time she didn't even think about it.

They entered a kitchen that was clearly well used. A cutting board with remnants of mushrooms and tomato slices sat on the granite topped island in the middle of the room. There were a few dirty dishes in the sink and she scented various spices. A man who could cook? Damn, why did she find that so sexy?

When Grant slid her package of cookie dough into the stainless steel refrigerator she noticed a plate of obviously homemade cookies on the counter next to it. She winced, feeling a little silly at bringing over the package and must have made a sound because he glanced over his shoulder then tracked her gaze.

His lips quirked. "My brother's fiancé made those. She's always sending food over here. You can have one."

Grabbing one, she followed him out onto his back porch where the mother of all grills sat. The built-in contraption was bigger than her stove and the steel blended with the stone so it wasn't gaudy or out of place. "My brothers would consider killing you for that thing," she murmured before taking a bite of the cookie—then made a mental note to snag a couple before she left.

Keeping his right side to her, Grant grinned as he opened the lid. "Yeah, I think my own brothers have considered it a time or two. Neither of their women will let them buy something 'so ridiculous', and I'm quoting both of them."

Six burgers, multiple links of kielbasa and bright colored vegetables on grill sticks lined the top rack in perfectly even rows. Her eyes widened a fraction. Good Lord, the man hadn't been kidding when he said he'd been planning to grill. "How many brothers do you have?"

"Two. Both older."

"They're the ones in the photos I saw on the way in?" Belle took a seat at one of the cushioned chairs underneath a square patio table. The sage green umbrella gave her relief from the sun.

He nodded as he fiddled with one of the knobs. "Yeah. You said you have brothers?"

"Yep. Three of them and they're all older too."

Grant shot her a look she couldn't quite describe as he lowered the lid. It wasn't exactly heated, but she was under the impression he was checking her out and not in a neighborly fashion. Unlike when Paulos looked at her with male interest, she found she liked being under Grant's scrutiny.

"I imagine they're all overprotective," he said quietly.

She grinned. "Yes and it's incredibly annoying. When I was in high school it was impossible to date."

He gave her another look and this time there was no doubt of the frank male interest in his gaze. She was surprised by the way her throat seized. Belle never had a problem talking and male interest was something she'd been dealing with since she was fifteen. If anything, she usually couldn't shut up. Right now she couldn't formulate anything coherent. She was too caught up in the blue storm of his eyes.

When he cleared his throat she was able to break contact. Even so, that deep voice of his sent a shiver twining through her when he said, "Do you want something to drink? I'm sorry I didn't offer you anything before. I've got beer and...water." He grimaced slightly, the action softening his features even as the scars on the side of his face pulled tight. It also highlighted his lips. A man should not have such soft, inviting lips. They seemed so out of place with his harsh, almost sharp features and large build.

And there went that strange flip-flop sensation in her belly. It was so easy to fantasize what it would feel like to have those strong hands and very kissable lips on her. What was wrong with her? She couldn't be having sexual thoughts about her neighbor. "Beer sounds great." It was Friday, why not?

When he opened a door on the right side of the grill underneath a long, flat surface likely used for preparing food, she was surprised to see a mini-fridge. Yeah, her brothers would totally kill for this thing. After popping the top, he handed her a Corona and when their fingers brushed, she felt a little spark arc between them. Forcing herself to ignore the heat working its way down her body to the juncture between her thighs she said, "So how long have you lived here?"

"Few years. It's a nice area, quiet for the most part."

She snorted. "Until I disturbed your peace."

Grinning in that sexy way she was coming to enjoy watching, he sat across from her. "Who was that guy and why was he grabbing you like that?" There was no joking in his voice now. Just a serious, deadly calm.

Okay then. He wasn't going to be polite and ignore what he'd seen and that made her respect him more. Even if it also made her uncomfortable. Clasping the cold beer in her hands, she balanced it on her bare leg. She cleared her throat as she picked at the label. "Are you sure you want to hear all this?"

"Yes." No room for argument in that deep voice.

Damn. She was hoping he'd let it go and she could just pretend to be his normal neighbor. Under any other circumstances she wouldn't tell a virtual stranger anything about her family or personal life, but Grant had put himself in between her and Paulos without her having to ask—not that she ever would have intentionally involved him. She felt like she owed him an explanation. "My family and Paulos's parents—the Balis's—have been friends forever. Our grandparents actually came over from Greece together. I...I don't even know how to explain it really because it's so stupid. Our parents have joked since we were kids that once he and I got married our two families will finally be related. I don't know what his deal is but it's like he's gotten it into his head that we *are* supposed to be together regardless of what *I* want. He took me off guard this morning but I'm not stupid. I'm not going to ignore this but I'm also not involving the police or anything. I'm going to talk to my mom about it and she'll talk to my dad and...his family will take care of him."

Grant was silent, those fathomless blue eyes looking at her. It was as if he could see inside her, see every little thing she was thinking. That was slightly terrifying. Finally he spoke again. "Do you have a security system?"

She shook her head. Belle had lived with her family for so long, even through college, because that's just the way things were done in her family. She'd never thought about things like security systems.

"I can get someone to install one—top of the line—at a deep discount." For some reason, it didn't really sound like he was asking. Though it wasn't exactly a command either.

She wasn't sure how she felt about that. What she did know was that she liked the way his voice sent pleasurable shivers spiraling through her body. And she was so thankful she had a bra on. Her nipples ached and seemed to flare to life every time he spoke. "Thanks."

He just nodded in acknowledgment and made a sort of grunting sound. Silence stretched between them and she couldn't seem to tear her gaze away from his. The way he watched her was almost curious but she couldn't miss the hint of lust there. Worse, she very much reciprocated. Which was stupid considering she barely knew him. But God, the man just exuded a raw power that turned her on. She knew it was purely physical. The guy was huge with incredibly broad shoulders and a muscled chest that couldn't be hidden under his shirt. She might have been in a slight state of shock earlier, but she hadn't missed all the ridges and planes of his body.

Even thinking about seeing him half-dressed again—
or completely undressed—was stupid. The couple she'd
bought the house from told her everyone in the neighborhood owned. No renters. Clearly he didn't plan on
leaving anytime soon and neither did she. Being attracted to the brooding man next door? That was okay. Acting on it? Most definitely not.

When he finally tore his gaze away and headed for
the grill she let out a pent up breath she hadn't realized
she'd been holding. Taking a long swig of her beer, she
forced herself not to look at Grant's very firm ass. Or
how big his hands were as he picked up a grilling utensil.

Shutting her eyes, she tried to banish the image of
those hands and force herself to stop imagining what it
would feel like to have them stroking her naked skin,
but it was no use. Belle wanted her neighbor and now
that she was finally out from the ridiculously overprotective tendencies of her brothers and parents, she *really*
wanted to go for it. Even if it would come back to bite
her in the ass later.

CHAPTER TWO

Using the shadows as cover, he grasped the top of the seven foot privacy fence and pulled himself up. Propelling himself over, he landed in Belle Manikas's backyard with a soft thud.

He waited a moment. A dog barked a few houses away, though he wasn't sure of the direction. Must be damn annoying for the neighbors at three in the morning. Other than that sound, there were a few crickets but nothing else in the immediate vicinity.

Her house was almost completely dark except for a dim light in one of the upstairs bedrooms. Her room, he figured, since he hadn't actually been in the house.

Yet.

But there was no visible movement in the room. Not that it mattered. He loved it when his victims struggled. He planned to make this kill quicker than normal. After having his fun with her, he'd strangle and leave her naked and splayed out in her backyard for her neighbor to find.

Normally he liked to take his dates back to his soundproofed playroom. But not this one. She was special.

She was a message to someone.

The overgrown rosebushes and untrimmed hedge cloaked him as he crept silently along the edge of the fence until he was close to the corner of her house. He'd loosened the floodlights on her back porch the day before because breaking them would have been too obvious. It had been a risk doing it during the daytime but she was worth it. Still, he wanted to test them before moving any closer.

With gloved hands, he pulled out a small, newly planted hydrangea bush. The root was thick with soil. Tossing it at the porch, he smiled when it hit the stone patio with a thud. The soil scattered everywhere but no flood of light.

Perfect.

Sticking to the shadows, he crept closer until he stood right at the French doors that led into the kitchen. Belle could have a security system, but he hadn't seen any signs on the doors or windows broadcasting that the house was protected. The last time he'd peeked through her windows, he hadn't seen any sensors either. He'd find out soon enough if he was right. Pulling out his lock pick kit, he made quick work of the pathetic barrier.

His heart pounded wildly against his chest and his palms were damp inside his gloves. He always got like this before a kill. Watching the life drain out of someone at his own hands was the best thrill. He'd tried to find a substitute, something else to fill the dark void inside him, but nothing worked.

Hand on the slim nickel colored door handle, he froze when a bright light hit him in the side of the face.

Blind with panic, he let go of the handle when he heard *him*.

"What the fuck are you doing?" Grant *fucking* Caldwell shouted as he flashed the brightest damn flashlight in his face from over the fence.

Without pausing or answering, he turned and sprinted back the way he'd come. He knew the former detective was still recovering and suffered from a limp. The man wouldn't be able to follow him and that was his only saving grace.

He raced across the yard, his heart pounding against his ribcage. The beam from the flashlight bounced off him and the fence he was narrowing in on, but he forced himself to funnel out the shouting behind him.

Once he cleared the fence he didn't stop running. He just kept on until he reached the vehicle he'd stashed two blocks over. Sparing a glance behind him, he let out a shaky breath as he started the engine.

He'd stolen the older model truck, but he'd still ditch it as soon as he was in the heart of Miami. Just in case that bastard had somehow scaled the fence and followed after him, he couldn't risk Caldwell calling in the license plate.

He'd been too careful to get caught now. Toying with the former detective would just have to wait. He'd been fucking with Caldwell for a while now. Just because the detective thought he could retire didn't mean *he* was done playing.

* * *

Belle raced down her stairs, uncaring about her state of undress. She wasn't sure what was going on, but she'd seen Grant chasing after a masked man in her backyard. Adrenaline punched through her, like an actual physical blow to her body.

Hurrying through the house and flipping on lights as she went, she stopped only after realizing one of the French doors in her kitchen was slightly ajar.

Panic gripped her heart in a tight fist. She could see the light from a flashlight dancing across her fence, but for some reason her floodlights weren't on. She tried the switch by the door, but it didn't help. When the flashlight suddenly turned off, she had to fight back full blown terror. Was the intruder coming back for her?

Taking a tentative step outside, she blinked, trying to adjust to the darkness. A few neighbors had lights on in their backyards—including Grant's house—but her backyard was filled with trees and bushes, eclipsing everything in darkness.

"Grant?" she called out, fearful for him.

"I'm here." His deep voice soothed her even though she couldn't see him.

A few seconds later his large, broad form emerged from the shadows near her back fence. He wore a long-sleeved black T-shirt and loose black sweatpants. Well, they weren't so loose as to hide his ridiculously muscular thighs. Her eyes traveled over his body, drinking in all that power before reality slapped her hard in the face. "What the hell is going on?"

Grant determinedly strode toward her, his slight limp emphasized. When he was only a few feet away she was able to see what she'd been missing before. He had a flashlight in one hand and a gun in the other.

Her eyes widened and she automatically took a step back. Not because she was afraid of him, but because clearly whatever was going on warranted a weapon. And why hadn't her motion-sensor lights gone off? "Are you okay?" she whispered.

Jaw tight, he nodded as he assessed her from head to foot. His look was completely non-sexual, almost clinical even, but her nipples strained against her thin tank top nonetheless. "I should be asking you that."

"Who was that?" She wasn't sure why she asked. There was no way he could know. The question just popped out from sheer nervousness.

Grant looked over his shoulder into the inky darkness then back at her. He motioned with his hand toward her house. "Come on. Let's get inside first."

Not seeing a point in arguing, she stepped back and turned the dimmer switch in her kitchen so that it wasn't so bright. It was too early and she was too shaken for the full bright lights of the room.

Wrapping her arms around herself, she waited until Grant closed and locked her door. He casually tucked his gun in the back of his pants then laid his flashlight on the small wood and tile-topped island in the middle of her kitchen. A few copper pots hung above it and he was so tall, his head cleared some of them. His face was grim when he looked at her. "Someone tried to break into your house tonight. Maybe you should tell me a little more about this Paulos." There was such a deadly edge to Grant's voice, she shivered.

The moment she did, he took a step forward, quickly covering the distance between them. His hand rested on her arm though he didn't completely pull her into a full embrace. Just lightly held her and watched her with those dark indigo eyes.

She blinked, trying to gather her wits. "My back door was open. Someone *did* break in," she said quietly.

When Grant's eyes narrowed, she felt the full impact of what he must have been like as a detective. He probably scared confessions out of people with just one look.

She understood on an intellectual level that the anger on his face wasn't directed at her, but unable to stop herself, she turned away. Looking toward her now locked back door, she realized the flimsy lock was useless.

Someone had broken into her house and if it hadn't been for Grant, anything could have happened. She'd never lived on her own before until now and she'd always felt safe because she had locks on her windows and doors and lived in normal, quiet neighborhoods. Clearly none of that mattered. Another shiver racked her body and this time Grant pulled her into a tight embrace.

Wanting to feel his strength, she slid her arms around his waist and held tight. His chin rested on the top of her head and he murmured soothing sounds as he stroked a hand down her spine. After a few minutes she felt something strong and insistent pressing against her belly. Grant stiffened as if he was suddenly aware of it too—well, he should be—but didn't pull away.

Maybe it should have startled her, but Belle wasn't bothered by it. As a nurse she understood it was biology. He'd just gotten what amounted to a shot of adrenaline and getting an erection was within the normal range of side effects and well…okay, it startled her a little. The feel of that hard length against her was unnerving, but not in a scary way. No, definitely not that. It unnerved her because she liked the feel of it and wondered if maybe it wasn't from the adrenaline but her. Clearly she had issues.

"I'm sorry," he muttered eventually and took a step back.

The timing was inappropriate but she let out a brief chuckle that seemed to dispel whatever tension was in the room. Using willpower she didn't realize she had, she kept her gaze on his face. "How did you... What happened exactly?"

Grant's jaw was still impossibly tight as he motioned for her to sit at the island. Perching on the edge of one of the high-backed wooden chairs, she watched him move around her kitchen with a fluid grace. As if he belonged there.

With his back to her, he pulled down a glass and started to fill it with ice from her freezer as he began to speak. "After that run in with your family friend today I decided to keep an eye on your house tonight. Some guys just don't know how to take no for an answer." He shook his head as he grabbed a can of soda from the fridge. "Whoever he was, the guy was quiet and he knew how to blend in. If I hadn't been watching your house so damn intently I might not have seen him." He slid the glass in front of her. "Drink. It'll help with the shock of adrenaline."

The liquid was blessedly cool as it rolled down her throat. After a few long swallows she set it down and clasped her shaking hands tightly in her lap. She didn't think it was Paulos breaking in to her house. He was annoying and a bit of a bully, but she couldn't see him trying to actually hurt her. Not like this. And it wasn't as if she had any enemies. Well, not that she knew of. Her family all had normal, respectable jobs so she couldn't imagine being targeted or singled out because of a familial relationship. For once in her life, however, she was absolutely speechless.

"Belle? Talk to me." Grant pulled up one of the chairs and sat so that their knees were touching. The contact sent a jolt of raw awareness through her. It brought her back to reality in a way a sugar rush from a soda never could.

"I'm fine." She was thankful she'd found her voice. "Really shaken up, but...what do we do now?" The thought of calling the cops when nothing had been taken seemed almost stupid, but...

"I'm going to call my former partner in on this. Hopefully you won't have to go down to the station to make a statement tonight, but you need to make a report."

"Did you—"

He seemed to read her mind as he shook his head. "Got a basic build and guesstimate on his height, but I didn't get a good look at him. He wore a mask, gloves and all black. Like a fucking ninja," Grant muttered, disgust lacing each word.

"Okay." She nodded, hating the numbness that welled up inside her. Belle had been so excited to move out on her own. She loved her family but they were overbearing and rarely *listened* to what she wanted. This place was supposed to be her safe haven. A place where all the other bullshit in her life just faded into the background.

She vaguely listened as Grant made a phone call. He spoke in monosyllabic grunts, but apparently whoever was on the other end understood perfectly because when Grant hung up, he seemed relieved. "My friend is on his way. You won't have to leave your house tonight."

Relief welled up inside her, but it was short lived. Once his detective friend left, she'd be all alone. Sleep was out of the question. The thought of closing her eyes when some masked intruder had wanted into her house for God only knew what sort of purposes was terrifying.

"You can stay at my place or I'll sleep on your couch." Grant's voice was deep, intoxicating and it took a moment for his words to completely register.

It really was like the powerfully built man could read her mind. Part of her wanted to be annoyed at his high-handedness. But the other part—that was scared shit-less—was thankful he'd be close by. Despite the fact that someone had almost invaded her haven, she didn't want to go next door. She wanted to stay put and in a way, stand her ground. "Stay here. Please...and thank you."

Grant grunted a non-response and looked down at his phone, as if he couldn't face her. Though she couldn't imagine why. Hating the feeling that she'd somehow made him uncomfortable, she reached out and cupped his non-scarred cheek. The action was almost instinctual, which made no sense, considering they hadn't known each other very long.

To her surprise, he didn't pull away. Those mercurial eyes of his landed on hers and pinned her with a laser-like focus. Belle knew she shouldn't be feeling anything right now other than fear, but her entire body heated up.

Pleasurable tingles skittered through her, hitting all her nerve endings with the subtlety of a mallet striking a gong. She tried to order her hand to move, to let go, but instead she slid off her chair so that she was standing in between his massive legs.

His eyes widened slightly and when she moved her hand so that she was practically holding the back of his neck in a death grip, she didn't see surprise, but raw lust flare in those indigo depths.

Oh yeah, he wanted her. Which was good considering she was pretty much throwing herself at him. She'd never really taken charge before. Of course she'd never actually been in a real relationship before. Right now she wanted to straddle Grant and take charge in all sorts of wicked ways. From the dark, mesmerizing look he was raking over her face she had a funny feeling he'd let her do whatever she wanted. And then he'd do the same to her in turn. God, imagining the feel of his hands and mouth tracking over her naked body sent a delicious shiver rolling through her.

This one was so unlike the way she'd been shaking earlier. It had nothing to do with fear and everything to do with pleasure. Her eyelids became heavy as she narrowed in on Grant's lips. Lips that looked so soft, inviting and completely kissable.

Grant leaned forward, covering the short distance between them so that their lips were a fraction apart. His warm breath tickled her face, making heat pool between her legs.

"I don't want to take advantage of you," he said so softly it took a moment for her to register his words.

She wanted to laugh but knew the timing was inappropriate. She'd practically jumped on him. Still wanted to, and he was worried about taking advantage. Considering they were neighbors and this had disaster written all over it, she was tempted to stop and pull back. But God help her, she didn't want to. For once in her life she wanted to be reckless. Her lips tugged into a smile—and the doorbell rang.

Grant jerked back as if he'd been punched and let out a graphic curse. She let her hand drop but didn't move from the haven of his spread legs. Every instinct told her she could trust him and that was sexy in itself.

"That'll be Carlito." He pushed his chair back and stood.

Grant gave her one long, almost appraising look before something akin to disappointment covered his features. Then that damn mask fell back into place and she couldn't figure out what he was thinking at all.

Belle wanted to tell herself that the interruption was for the best. But Grant had this strange, intoxicating impact on her. When she was around him she didn't want to think about consequences. She just wanted that hot body of his on hers. Sighing, she raked a hand through her hair and followed after Grant. Time to deal with reality.

CHAPTER THREE

Grant transferred the bacon he'd cooked to a paper-towel covered plate. Though he'd hated to leave Belle for even a second, he'd gone home and grabbed some food from his refrigerator—since she had nothing in hers—so he could cook her breakfast. She'd still been sound asleep once he'd returned and he knew she probably needed it.

After Grant's former partner, Carlito Duarte, had left last night Belle had crashed. He'd seen the events of the night caving in on her as she'd been questioned and the second he'd locked up after Carlito, she'd made a beeline for her bedroom.

The fact that she'd come on to him last night and had been very intent on kissing him still stunned him. When he was with her, he forgot about his scars and limp. She didn't seem to notice so he didn't focus on them either. It was strange and freeing and...fucking scary. He'd never been in a long term or even short term relationship. It wasn't that he had issues with women. Hell, he loved them. They were soft, sexy and smelled great. His job had just never been conducive to anything long term. He worked nights, long hours and almost all holidays. Now he was jobless, had a fucked up face and body, and a gorgeous woman wanted him? Yeah, that was scary.

Of course he'd been very aware of his flaws when Carlito had shown up. His former partner was a pretty boy and never wanting for female companionship. Grant was straight but even he could appreciate the GQ thing Carlito had going on. While Grant had never had a problem getting laid before his accident, women just threw themselves at his friend. The guy didn't even have to try.

Which was why Belle's reaction to him last night had stunned Grant—and even though his friend would never admit it, her complete lack of awareness of Carlito, had taken the good detective off guard too.

She'd been practically sitting in Grant's lap last night as she'd answered question after question and even when his friend turned that trademark smile on her, Belle hadn't batted an eye or blushed or…anything. She'd just continued to look at Grant for support. Damn if that hadn't made him feel ten feet tall. All she had to do was turn those clear green eyes on him and he'd do anything for her.

"Something smells good." Belle's soft voice pulled him out of his thoughts. "Where'd you find bacon?"

Turning around, he found her standing in the entryway thankfully wearing a soft looking robe that fell to her ankles. Last night she'd been wearing body-hugging pajama shorts and a skin tight tank top that left little to the imagination. It was hard to focus on anything but her body when she was like that. Hell, even when she was covered like this it was hard to focus but at least all that gorgeous toned, tanned skin wasn't slapping him in the face.

"I grabbed some food from my house," he said quietly, not looking directly at her. Doing so was damn hard sometimes. She was just so pretty and even though he was able to forget about the way he looked sometimes, seeing her reminded him of his flaws. "The lack of food in your refrigerator is pathetic."

She chuckled lightly as she stumbled for the nearly full coffee pot. "I know. I just moved in though so cut me some slack." After pouring herself a mug, she came closer, closer yet, until she leaned against the counter right next to him.

She smelled so good it made him pause. The subtle scent of raspberries and vanilla tickled his nose. Probably the lotion she used. At least she wasn't on his scarred side. Still, with her sleepy eyes and hair tousled around her face like she'd just had sex, he wanted to drag his fingers through her long dark tresses and tug her close to him and make that just-had-sex-look a reality. No one had a right to look so hot in the morning, but even without makeup she looked fresh and damn if he didn't want to bury his face in the crook of her neck while he buried his cock in her wet heat. *Fuck.* What was wrong with him? She'd said something, he was sure of it. Clearing his throat, he said, "What?"

Her eyebrows drew slightly together. "I asked how you slept. Was my couch too uncomfortable? I still haven't bought furniture for my guest room but it's on my list."

The truth was he hadn't slept much at all, but she didn't need to know that. "It was perfect, but I think I should be asking you how you slept."

Her knuckles turned white as she grasped her mug and she shrugged in what he guessed she thought would come off as casual. In reality it was jerky, unsteady and made him want to tug her into a comforting embrace. "I slept okay. Not great, but...okay."

"Well you look great," he murmured, then wanted to kick himself. He hadn't meant to say that out loud.

Her cheeks flushed a beautiful shade of red, but she didn't avert her gaze. Just stared at him with big green eyes that he could drown in. And she didn't hide anything in her expression. That's what killed him. She wore her feelings and emotions right out in the open. He could actually see her lust and he didn't understand why she was attracted to him. He wasn't used to dealing with anyone so unguarded. Definitely not in his former profession and none of his brothers or his father were like that. He'd lost his mother at a young age and his dad had never remarried. Throw in all his years in the Marines and he wasn't exactly swimming in emotional awareness. He just couldn't wrap his mind around why she stared so openly.

Maybe it was because he'd saved her. But he didn't see gratitude right now. Just desire and need. It was like an electric, almost living thing between them. As if he could reach out and touch the heat simmering there. He swallowed hard, hating how out of depth he felt around her, when grease popped in the frying pan as the new strips of bacon he'd put in started sizzling.

Turning away from Belle, he welcomed the distraction of cooking. With the moment broken, she sighed and stepped back. As she started grabbing plates from one of the whitewashed cabinets, he couldn't help but watch her in his periphery. Just being around her was messing with his head. He couldn't think of anything but sex.

Raw, no holds barred, naked for hours and hours kind of sex. On the island top. On her couch. The stairs on the way up to her room. Or on that giant bed of hers with the ridiculous frilly throw pillows. But he didn't just want wild with her. He wanted soft and gentle. The thought of going down on her for hours, of taking his time with her, was mesmerizing. *Fuck me.* He'd always been a take it or leave it kind of guy when it came to sex. Around her, however, he felt like a maniac.

"Have you thought about going into work? Maybe it'll keep your mind off everything?" There. He could ask questions like a normal human being. Questions that did not involve asking her what her favorite sexual positions were.

Last night he'd found out that she worked as neonatal nurse but had taken a week off to settle into her house. When he'd been a detective he'd always used work as a distraction so it surprised him when she shook her head.

"No. I'm not giving some asshole control over my life. This is my house and I want to get settled in. I've still got a ton of stuff to buy and boxes to unpack. Besides, I need to see about getting an alarm system—"

"I've taken care of it. I called my brother Harrison this morning and told him to wire your house *today*."

Harrison had seemed strained, but Grant knew it wasn't directed at him. His brother had been crazy busy at work. Their father had started Red Stone Security years ago after retiring from the CIA. And he almost always hired former military men and women. Considering Harrison had just gotten married, Grant had a feeling his brother was trying to balance married life and a very demanding job.

"What does that mean? I need to shop around, figure out who I want to go with."

He snorted, knowing she'd end up with a standard three-year contract with a standard security company with a *standard* system that any decent thief could bypass. Um, no. "You ever heard of Red Stone Security?"

"Uh, yeah. Who hasn't? Keith Caldwell owns it. I think he used to work for the government but no one really knows for what branch. They guard all the special dignitaries and...*Caldwell.* Oh. My. God. You said you were a former detective." Her tone was slightly accusatory.

Grant slid the cooked bacon from the pan to join the others on the plate. "I am. Keith is my dad. You're correct in that they guard foreign dignitaries and pretty much anyone important who comes to Miami." And around the globe, but he didn't go into all that. "They also have a very small division for industrial security systems. You'll never find anything better." He opened the carton of eggs and glanced at her.

She sank on to one of the high-backed chairs, her expression pinched. He hated the way her face tightened. "I really appreciate that, but...I can't afford that. In fact, I think if you even tell me the ballpark range of what it costs I'll probably die from shock."

He frowned at her as he realized she'd misunderstood him. "You're not paying for it."

Belle blinked once as understanding set in. She slid off the chair, eyes flashing with annoyance. "Well you're certainly not."

He grunted. *We'll see about that.* "How do you like your eggs? I can do scrambled, fried or even make an omelet." He'd brought over mushrooms, a pepper and some cheese. Wouldn't be the best omelet, but it would do.

"Scrambled is fine...but you're not paying for my security system. That's just ridiculous!"

"Why? Consider it a welcome to the neighborhood gift." He didn't leave any room for argument in his voice. It was happening *today*. Some primal part of him he didn't really understand needed this woman safe.

"A plate of freshly baked cookies would be more appropriate." She sank back on to the seat, some of the steam leaving her, but he knew without a doubt this argument wasn't over.

He just didn't care. Yeah, he knew he was being a little bullish about it, but damn, the thought of her injured or attacked by some lunatic made him crazy. "If it makes you feel better I'm getting the family discount and it's mainly a selfish purchase."

"How on earth is it selfish?" she snapped, a bit of heat in her words that got him even hotter.

"I wouldn't be able to sleep at night worrying about you. Knowing you have a system by Red Stone will help me get my beauty sleep. And God knows I need it," he muttered the last part under his breath.

But she heard him. Sliding off her seat, she covered the small distance between them in a few strides. "What's that supposed to mean?"

Of course she wouldn't let it go. This woman was intoxicating, infuriating and too damn gorgeous for her own good. "Do you like cheese in your eggs?" God, he was a total coward but looking at her right now was out of the question. And answering her question? He felt like an ass for having said anything, but damn it, he knew what he looked like. More than anything he fucking *wanted* her to acknowledge it. Not look at him with wide, welcoming eyes.

Taking him by surprise, she reached up and grabbed his chin. Dropping the spatula in his hand, he had no choice but to turn to her. He could barely react as she practically lunged at him, her lips meeting his in a furious frenzy.

And he froze.

For a fraction of a second before he returned those heated kisses. She might have started it, but he took over. He couldn't help it. Blindly he reached out and turned off the knob on the stove. Then he slid his hands down her side until he clutched her ass and lifted her up.

His erection was huge and pressing right into the juncture between her thighs and she wasn't pulling away. Nope, she'd started grinding against him as if she couldn't get enough.

God, what was wrong with her? Why did she want him? She wrapped her legs around his waist as her fingers dug into his shoulders with an undeniable urgency. And her lips...they met his stroke for stroke, pushing, teasing and taking until finally he had to pull back.

Breathing hard, he looked down at her flushed face. Her lips were swollen, her eyes glazed and he could practically smell the desire coming off her it was so potent.

"Why do you want me?" he rasped out, hating the desperation in his voice but unable to stop it.

"Why wouldn't I? You have that whole sexy and powerful thing going on and you're clearly a good person. You came running over when Paulos went all crazy on me and...are you asking because of your scars?"

Unable to answer, he nodded as he took another step toward the island top with her still wrapped around him. He moved so that she was sitting but he stayed in between her legs as she lightly traced circles on his shoulders. She was silent for a long moment then finally one of her hands dropped. Belle drew open her robe then grabbed the middle of her tank top and yanked it down.

For a moment he forgot to breathe until he realized what she was doing. Revealing what all her tight tops had covered before. He frowned at the straight, dark pink scar running down the middle of her chest, the tiny marks showing where the staples had been. It was a perfect line and at least five inches from what he could see, probably longer. He'd seen this type of scar before. Considering the almost angry coloring and the surprising thickness of it, he guessed she'd gotten it when she was a kid. "Heart surgery?"

She nodded. "More than one."

"Are you—"

She released the material, covering breasts he hadn't gotten a good enough view of. "I'm fine and I don't want to talk about me right now. I want to talk about what's going on in your head. You think because you have some scars you're not attractive? Or what, that I feel sorry for you?" She snorted as if the thought was so ludicrous he had to be insane. Something warm spread across his chest as she continued. "You practically ooze sexual appeal. It's ridiculously frustrating being around you because you're so masculine and abrasive and a little bossy. And...I really like it. All I can seem to think about when I'm around you is kissing you. Well that and other stuff and I know I'm not supposed to just come out and admit that I think you're hot, but...I'm going to stop talking now before you get a big head."

Grant couldn't stop the bark of laughter that escaped. He leaned forward until his forehead was touching hers.

Belle had gotten under his skin without trying. She was so energetic and flirty and made him forget everything that had kept him so damn depressed these past six months. Part of him wondered if she had some sort of savior complex for him, but the selfish part of him ignored that thought.

Getting involved with his neighbor was monumentally stupid, but because it was Belle it was hard to care. As he leaned in to kiss her again, his phone buzzed in his pocket. Her leg was draped around his backside and she had to feel it.

They both froze. Groaning, she let her toned legs fall away from him. Her robe fell back into place, covering all that skin as she laid a hand on his chest. Her long fingers flexed once against him. "It could be your partner or someone about the break in."

He knew that, but it didn't quell the urge to disregard his phone. Sighing, he stepped away—ignoring his painful erection—and put some distance between them because if he was touching her, he wouldn't be concentrating on anything else. A quick glance at the caller ID confirmed that it was indeed his former partner. As he snapped open his phone, Belle shot him a look so heated he wanted to drop his cell and take her right there on the counter. But just as quickly she slid from her seat and refilled her coffee cup and the spell was broken.

* * *

Belle tried to ignore what Grant's mere presence did to her, but it was hard. She couldn't believe her sexy neighbor with shoulders so broad she wanted to nip, kiss and lick her way across them, had stayed the night to protect her *and* cooked her breakfast. In her giant family, the women were always expected to cook and serve the males and all that annoying stuff. It was maddening and was probably why she'd resisted learning everything her mother had wanted to teach her, namely cooking. She knew she drove her mother, grandmother and aunts crazy because of it. Just like she'd driven them crazy when she'd decided to go to nursing school. They'd all just expected her to skip college and work in one of her family's many businesses. While she loved her relatives dearly she'd needed something that was all hers.

Not to mention she loved her job. Working with babies all day was a dream come true. She could work with all that cuteness, but not actually deal with a baby or kids at home. She wanted one someday but she was still enjoying her youth. Of course no job was perfect. Some days were depressing as hell, but the good definitely outweighed the bad. Sort of like this morning. She should be reeling from the attempted break in—and she sort of was—but all she could seem to focus on was images of Grant naked. Or what she *imagined* he would look like. The feel of his erection just minutes before had her coming up with all sorts of goodness.

As soon as he shut his phone, she shoved those images aside. "What's going on?"

"Well, Paulos Balis," Grant said the man's name with barely concealed disgust, "has an alibi. Don't know how strong it is, but supposedly he stayed the night at his parents and his mother was up late enough to allegedly know he was home around the time someone was breaking into your home."

Belle jumped at the sound of her house phone ringing. It was in the receiver on the wall by the fridge. "Hold on." She glanced at the caller ID. *Her mother.* Yeah, Belle had known that was coming. Now that Paulos had been questioned by the police, she had a feeling she'd be getting an unexpected visit soon. Probably from half her family. *Just great.* Turning the ringer off, she ignored it and sat back down. "What else did he say?"

"No break-ins in the area recently and basically no leads." Grant grimaced, as if was his fault.

She rubbed a hand over her face, trying to digest everything and ignore the fact that her mother would be by shortly. Hell, probably her brothers too. And she so didn't need to be here for that. "When are your guys coming to install that security system?"

His eyebrows rose and something like victory flashed across his face. She knew she shouldn't give in to him, but she'd be paying him back for it. She didn't know how, but she definitely would. At the moment, she didn't want to argue with anyone. She just wanted to get the hell out of her house in case her mother made a surprise visit.

"About noon," Grant said.

That gave her a few hours. "I need to run some errands, stop by a furniture store, the grocery store and—"

"I'll go with you."

She blinked once, surprised. "That's not necessary."

"I know. Maybe I just want to spend time with you." He turned the stove back on, but shot her an unreadable look over his shoulder before turning back to the uncooked eggs.

"No one likes furniture or grocery shopping." And in her experience, especially men.

He just shrugged those impossibly broad shoulders and she knew insisting she wanted to go by herself was an argument she'd lose. The truth was, the thought of spending the morning with Grant was wildly appealing. So much so, she was starting to worry a little about what she'd gotten herself into.

CHAPTER FOUR

Belle peered out the window of Grant's kitchen into his expansive backyard. His giant pool glistened under the afternoon sun. Sparkly and oh so cool. It practically beckoned to her. Florida was notoriously humid and even though they lived near the Atlantic, sometimes the heat was smothering. Of course she was inside where the air conditioning was blessedly running overtime, but she wanted to test out his pool in a bad way.

After hours of shopping—and spending way too much of her savings on furniture and kitchen stuff—she and Grant had returned home to find men waiting for her to let them in to install her brand new security system. They were still next door covering all her doors and windows with sensors, even the ones upstairs, which seemed a little excessive, but Grant had been insistent. She'd tried broaching the subject of paying him again but he'd been completely dismissive. If her sexy neighbor hadn't been such a good shopping companion all morning she might have pushed him a little harder. But the thought of arguing with Grant left her feeling cold.

So now she was stuck inside Grant's house because he'd been called away by one of his brothers. Some family emergency that he hadn't wanted to talk about. But his grave expression had told her that family was the only thing that would have taken him away. She appreciated everything he was doing for her even if it did make her feel a little uncomfortable, but she just wanted to go home.

Some random guy had tried to break into her house. It wasn't as if she had a stalker or anything. The more time that passed the better she felt about the whole situation. Yes, it still freaked her out that someone had wanted to rob her or possibly worse. And she was thankful for the new sense of security, but it wasn't necessary to stay cooped up in Grant's house in broad daylight until he returned home. That was definitely overkill and if she let this man start running roughshod over her now it would never end. It's not like they were even in a relationship, but she could envision that as a possibility, and she couldn't let him make decisions for her.

She'd only recently stood up to her own family. With so many health and heart problems growing up, she understood why they'd been so over-protective but at twenty-four, it had been time to move out. At first her mother had been horrified—and though she wouldn't admit it, secretly impressed when Belle had put a big down payment on her new house with her own money—but eventually her mom and the rest of the family had come around. It wasn't like they could keep her a freaking prisoner.

Which was sort of how she felt now. Being trapped in this strange house brought up too many familiar negative feelings. Giving the pool a longing look, she made a decision. She hurried next door and politely announced her presence to the men working, and tried not to stare at the man with the mohawk, piercings and numerous tattoos because if he worked for Red Stone and Grant trusted him, then she would too. He didn't give her the creeps, he was just visually intimidating as hell and she'd had a rough enough night.

After packing a small bag with her bathing suit, sunscreen lotion and a change of clothes, she headed back to Grant's. She was still doing what he said, but getting in a few laps and stretching her legs couldn't harm anything. It was the middle of the day and she had full visibility of his entire backyard. Unlike hers with tons of bushes and places to hide, his was wide open.

She quickly changed into her checkered green and blue two-piece bathing suit then pulled her hair back into a tight ponytail. The moment she descended the short set of stairs into the shallow end, she pushed out a sigh of relief. The cool water lapped against her bare legs, then stomach until she fully immersed herself. Yeah, this was exactly what she'd been craving.

Doing the breast stroke, she cut through the water with even, steady strokes, hitting the wall at the deep end, then returning to the shallow end. Over and over, she kept swimming until her muscles burned.

She wasn't sure how long she'd been in the pool but the warm sun beating on her back and her tired body told her it was time to get out. As she reached the wall in the deep end, she was ready to push off for her last lap when she glimpsed a masked figure in her line of sight. She blinked trying to get the water out of her eyes when strong hands shoved her under.

Belle tried to suck in a breath but pulled in water, burning her nose and throat. Choking and thrashing around, she grasped at the forearms of the man holding her under water. And there was no doubt it was a man. His hands were really strong and holy shit, she was going to die. The thought registered clearly in her fogged mind.

She kicked out her legs but wasn't close to reaching the bottom. Terror burst inside her as she continued to struggle. A raw kind of fear slithered into her bloodstream. Her toes connected with the wall, the pain jarring her straight to her bones.

Reaching up she grasped onto the man's forearm and raked her fingers down his skin. She could feel his entire body jolt at that. She inwardly cheered that she'd injured him.

One of his hands loosened. Before she could strike again, she was jerked above the surface. Sucking in a breath, she struggled to see her attacker but a hard fist connected with her jaw. A kaleidoscope of colors burst behind her eyelids as pain ricocheted through her.

Everything went fuzzy, but at least she could breathe. Then she was once again submerged into the cool depths. She tried to scratch him again but he kept pushing her down farther and farther. She couldn't get a grip on him, the wall, nothing.

Despair welled inside her as she began losing consciousness. She fought it, her brain screaming at her to hang on, fight harder, but she couldn't breathe. She wasn't sure how long she'd been submerged but her lungs burned and ached with pressure. With the desperate need for oxygen.

Darkness edged her vision and her eyes slowly drifted shut. The hands on her shoulders loosened and she started sinking. Deeper, deeper, her body floated weightless. Then a sharp tug on her arm jerked her back closer to consciousness but she couldn't open her eyes.

She was being propelled upward. In the distance she heard a man shouting. At her? She couldn't tell. There was another male voice. This one sounded like it was coming from a tunnel.

Someone opened her mouth and put their lips over hers. The rush of air into her lungs had her gasping for breath. Despite feeling like sandbags weighed on her eyelids she cracked her eyes open.

She thrashed out, rolling over as she coughed up water onto the concrete. Her palm slapped against it once as she tried to steady herself, but her stomach heaved and her nose burned as she spit out more water.

The guy with the mohawk was dripping wet and crouching next to her, concern on his face. "Are you okay?"

Turning so she could fully see him, she blinked once and nodded. Slowly moving her head, she attempted to look at her surroundings. Mohawk must have pulled her from the pool and laid her by the edge. The other technician was kneeling about a foot away from her head, his expression just as worried.

"What...happened?" she croaked, her voice raspy, throat raw and burning from the chlorine.

Mohawk's expression darkened and he exchanged a look with his partner before looking back at her. "Don't worry about it. We've called the cops and—"

"What happened?" she demanded as she tried to sit up. Her heart thudded overtime.

The moment she shifted, pain shot through her jaw, reminding her she'd been punched. And her feet hurt something fierce. Her toes were raw and bloody but she tried to ignore them. She wanted answers.

Sighing, the dripping man put an arm under her shoulders and helped her sit up straight. "Think you can stand?" he asked softly.

She nodded but when she tried to get up, even with his help, her knees gave way. God, she felt like such a wimp but her body just refused to obey. It was like her limbs were made of boiled linguini.

Cursing, the guy scooped her up and strode toward Grant's patio table and chairs. Gently he set her down on one of the cushioned chairs. Then he hovered and stared at her as if he was afraid she'd break.

"What's your name?" she finally asked.

For a moment he looked confused, as if she'd stunned him. "What?"

"Uh, name? I can't keep calling you Mr. Mohawk in my head," she said then wished she'd remembered to turn her filter on.

The guy's eyes widened as he let out a bark of laughter. "Uh, I'm Travis Sanchez and this," he motioned to the tall black man in the same uniformed shirt who'd been quiet, "is Vincent Hansen."

She nodded at both of them as an uncontrollable shiver raked through her. Hating the lack of control she suddenly experienced, she wrapped her arms around herself in an attempt to still her shaking but it was impossible. "What happened? And where's Grant?" Her teeth chattered so she clenched her jaw, aiming for more control.

Travis sat down in a chair across from her, but Vincent disappeared into Grant's house. "Some guy with a black mask tried to drown you. I saw someone jump Grant's fence while I was working on one of the windows. I got here as soon as I could. We managed to scare him off but—God, if I hadn't been working on that side of the house..." He scrubbed a hand over his face.

Belle reached out and patted his other hand shakily, feeling a little foolish at comforting him when her insides felt as if they'd split apart any second now. What the hell was happening? Someone had tried to drown her? Why? "I scratched the guy," she blurted as the horrifying experience played over in her head.

Travis's head snapped up at her words. "Good. Don't wash your hands. When the paramedics and detectives arrive we'll have them take samples. Maybe you got his DNA."

"Paramedics? I don't need to see anyone." She just wanted a hot bath then some dry clothes. And to get warm. Despite the sunshine, her teeth were chattering, her skin covered with goose bumps.

But Travis wasn't listening. He stood when Vincent approached, having retrieved a handful of towels. She sat numbly while he wrapped one around her. Tugging it tighter against her shoulders, she desperately tried to digest everything that had just happened while fighting the sudden onslaught of tears. More than anything, she just wished Grant was here. Had they called him? She wanted to ask, but knew if she opened her mouth again, tears would soon follow. While she really did love her family and knew they only wanted what was best for her, she knew they'd try to pack her up and move her back to her parents' home if she called them. Grant wouldn't do any of that. He always seemed so in control over every situation and right now she wouldn't mind some of his strength.

When men in uniform stormed the backyard she flinched when she realized she knew one of the paramedics from work. Great. The last thing she wanted was for the entire hospital to know her business.

Even worse, Grant was going to think she was some sort of lunatic who'd dumped all this drama into his life. She knew that was the last thing on earth she should be worried about, but the thought accosted her nonetheless. As one of the paramedics sat in front of her and began asking her questions, she fought back the tears that wanted to escape and focused all her attention on answering coherently. The last thing she was doing was going to the hospital and she knew that either the paramedics or one of the detectives she'd seen milling around the pool would try to push the issue.

Jeez, it was like they'd called out everyone from the Miami Police Department. Yeah, Grant was definitely going to regret talking to his new neighbor now. And she really couldn't blame him.

* * *

Grant jerked his truck to a halt as he hit the curb in front of his house. A handful of black and whites with their lights on were in his driveway and in Belle's. There was also an ambulance and Carlito's car along the curb. As he stormed across his front yard a rookie who looked like it was his first day out of the academy tried to stop him by holding out a hand.

"I live here," Grant snarled, bypassing the guy and ignoring his protests. As he reached the front door it flew open. Carlito's face was grim, making Grant's heart seize. Travis had called him and told him Belle was okay, but his former partner looked like death. "What the fuck is it? Is she hurt?"

"Nothing that won't heal. Her jaw, shoulders and neck are bruised. Her feet are a little raw, but she'll be fine. Physically anyway," Carlito talked as they hurried through his house. "She scratched the guy though. Got enough to run his DNA."

Grant paused, sucking in a deep breath. That was actually good news even if he hated that the guy had been close enough for her to touch. Travis had told him a masked man—just like last night—had tried to drown Belle. In *his* pool. What the hell was going on? And why had Belle been outside in the first place?

Sidestepping a paramedic walking through his back door, he scanned his backyard in seconds, quickly narrowing in on Belle. She sat with a giant blanket wrapped around her on one of his patio chairs. She was talking to Travis but her face was pale. When she saw him her eyes lit up. The sight was like a punch to the gut. She lifted a hand, half-waving, and her blanket fell open revealing that she was wearing a skimpy two-piece bathing suit. Okay, it was actually more than decent but he froze at all that skin.

Next to him Carlito hissed in a breath but Grant ignored him. He didn't have a claim on Belle. Stalking toward her, he stopped when he was right in front of her and kneeled down.

"Why the fuck were you outside?" He cringed the moment he barked the question. She blanched as if he'd struck her and he wanted to kick his own ass. "I'm sorry. That came out wrong... How are you doing?"

She took a shuddering breath and to his complete and utter surprise, lunged at him, wrapping her arms around his neck. Her blanket sagged and before he could shoot Travis a beseeching look the other man had grabbed it and was holding it against her back. Belle mumbled nonsensical words as she started crying. Real, gut-wrenching tears. Shit. Carlito and Travis had both told him she'd been keeping it together. His heart ached at seeing her falling apart like this. Sweet, funny Belle in tears made him want to kill whoever had done this. Grant had always been in control of his emotions but right now he felt positively murderous.

Lifting her up in his arms, he glanced around to find everyone staring at them. He wanted to shout at them to mind their own business but had a feeling that would upset Belle even more. Travis draped the blanket over her and Grant held onto it as best he could while holding her. He could barely understand what she was saying as she cried into his neck, but he was pretty sure she was apologizing. For what, he couldn't imagine.

He headed back for his house, only stopping to talk to Carlito and tell him to make sure everyone was gone as soon as possible. Considering the paramedic had left Belle he figured she wasn't going to the hospital, but he needed to confirm it anyway. As he hurried up his stairs he asked, "Did they say anything about you needing to go to the hospital?"

She shook her head almost violently and pulled back, her green eyes shimmering with tears. "I'm not going." There was a bite of attitude in her words and he was glad.

"They've taken the DNA from under your fingers, right?" he asked for clarification.

When she nodded he figured that was all he was getting from her. Striding to his bedroom, he shut the door behind them and put her on her feet. She wrapped her arms around herself but she seemed steady enough to stand on her own.

Grant nodded toward his open bathroom door. "I think you'll feel better if you take a bath or a hot shower. Are you okay to start it on your own?"

She just nodded again, her green eyes huge and terrified, her face an ashen gray and panic punched him in the chest. He wondered if she'd gone into shock. "Belle! You've got to give me some audible answers."

Belle pushed out a long sigh. "I'm...fine." Her breath hitched once. "When I saw you I guess I lost it. I'm so sorry. I'm officially the worst neighbor ever."

Frowning, he reached out and pulled her into a gentle hug, resting his chin on her head. He was just glad she was all right. Her hair smelled like chlorine and something fruity. "Honey, you have nothing to be sorry for. Some asshole attacked you in the middle of the day. There's no way any of us could have seen this coming." He refrained from giving her hell about going outside. It would be cruel and unnecessary considering what she'd already suffered.

She rubbed her face against his chest and wrapped her arms around him. When she did, the blanket that had been barely hanging on pooled at her feet. He wanted to make a grab for it, but didn't want to take his arms away from her. Gently he rubbed her back until she eventually stepped away, sniffling but not crying.

With strength he didn't realize he had, he kept his gaze averted from her mostly bare body. Looking over at his king-sized bed—which actually made things worse because all he could think about was her stretched out on it, completely naked and his face between her legs— he rubbed a hand over his face. "I'm going downstairs to talk to Carlito and get everyone cleared out of here. You're sure you're okay to take a shower on your own?"

"I'm good, I promise. Just sore, but that's okay," she said softly.

Throat tight, he nodded once then let himself out. He'd never experienced such raw terror in his life. He and Belle had just started getting to know one another. She was gorgeous, sure, but she was so sweet and funny. Imagining a world without her in it was impossible. He grabbed the door handle, not wanting to leave her, but when he heard the shower start he froze. The image of her completely naked was too much for his brain to handle. After getting his breathing under control, he headed downstairs.

One thing was clear. Whoever had attacked Belle hadn't picked her randomly. And the fact that her attacker had come after her in the middle of the day said a lot about his arrogance and his intent to kill her.

Grant had officially taken a job at Red Stone Security today after ironing out all the details with his father and brother, Harrison. Now he knew what his first job would be. Belle might not be a dignitary or have any political pull and definitely wasn't their normal type of client, but until they figured out who was after her, she was officially under his protection. Whether she liked it or not.

That wasn't why he'd left Belle today though. His brother Harrison had needed to talk. Grant had never heard his brother sound so damn desperate but something was going on with him and his new wife, Mara, so Grant had gone to talk things out with him. Dealing with his new job stuff had been secondary and now he hated that he'd been gone when he should have been watching a woman who was starting to mean way too much to him.

CHAPTER FIVE

Belle stared almost blindly at the row of feminine products. While she'd been a little leery of leaving the house only two days after her attack she'd realized it was the best thing for her sanity. She started back to work the upcoming weekend and needed a sense of normalcy in her life before then. Plus she was *not* sending Grant inside the grocery store to buy her tampons.

He'd been a little edgy about her going into the store by herself, but he'd dropped her off right at the front and it was the middle of the freaking day. Well, that didn't mean much anymore considering someone had tried to drown her during daylight hours, but at least here she was surrounded by a ton of people.

When she spotted her normal brand, she grabbed the pink box and tossed it into her basket. While she was here she might as well pick up some chocolate too. Her refrigerator was nearly empty but she always had to have that on hand.

As she neared the end of the aisle she jerked to a halt when Paulos Balis strode around the corner. He headed right for her and there was no mistake she was the reason for his presence. *He* certainly didn't need anything from this aisle.

Stopping when he was only a foot away, he glowered down at her, his dark eyes blazing with fury. She hated that he was so much taller and bigger than her. "You called the fucking cops on me?" he growled.

Oh, hell no. "Are you *stalking* me? How'd you know I'd be here?" Belle glanced around, fighting the nervousness shimmying through her. The aisle was empty but she could hear people the next aisle over. One good scream and Paulos would back off. Or maybe she'd strike him in the face with her basket if he didn't leave her alone.

He ignored her questions and took another subtle step closer, clearly trying to intimidate her with his size. "Why the hell did you call the cops?"

She held her basket in front of her, using it as a barrier. Even though she wanted to, she refused to take a step back. Paulos was a bully and she wasn't going to put up with his crap even if it did feel like her insides were actually shaking. "*Someone* tried to break into my house, which you already know." The cops had no doubt told him.

At first she'd been absolutely sure that Paulos hadn't been involved in the attempted break-in, but after nearly being drowned by a strong, *tall*—according to Vincent and Travis—assailant so soon after she didn't trust anyone. Especially not the very tall, angry man standing in front of her.

"And you think I had something to do with that?" he snarled, reaching out as if to grab her arm.

She tensed and actually took a step back. At the last second he dropped his hand, clearly thinking better of it. Before she could respond, he continued. "My fucking parents are giving me so much grief about the cops showing up to question me. What the hell is wrong with you?"

Her eyes widened. "*Me?* You show up at my house uninvited and try to manhandle me into...I don't even know what your intentions were. You're lucky my brothers don't know about what happened." This time she didn't hold back any of her anger.

His glare transformed into a sneer. "I never would have hurt you. Looks like you don't mind getting roughed up a little though," he said nastily as he nodded to her bruised jaw, obviously curious about it. There was such a dark edge to his words it took her off guard. As if he liked seeing her hurt.

Belle had used cover-up, but there was only so much makeup could do. She narrowed her eyes at him, wanting to lash out. Somehow she managed to hold onto a sliver of her control. She hadn't told her family what had happened in Grant's pool and she couldn't let her anger get the best of her. If she did, Paulos would gleefully tell her entire family what had happened. He knew how much she hated her family's constant hovering and would take great pleasure in annoying her out of spite. "I don't have time for your crap. The cops will leave you alone as long as you stay the hell away from me." She steered things back in the original direction of their conversation. To the reason he'd apparently ambushed her in the middle of the feminine hygiene product aisle. "And you never answered how you *knew* I'd be here?"

"I was on my way to your place when I saw you leaving the neighborhood with that guy." Paulos's face darkened at his reference to Grant.

"That guy? You mean my neighbor?"

"Yes! That bastard had no right to interrupt us during a private conversation. So now what? You're friends with him? Is he the one who smacked you around?" There was no concern in his question, only scorn and contempt.

"You're an idiot, Paulos. Now get out of my way before I scream or call the cops. I bet your mother would love to come bail you out of jail because you're stalking her friend's daughter."

His face turned a mottled red. "I swear to God, Belle—"

"You swear, what, Mr. Balis?" Grant strode up behind Paulos so quietly Belle hadn't even heard him move.

They were about a quarter of the way down the aisle and she'd been so focused on Paulos that she hadn't been paying attention to anything else. Paulos was tall and he'd blocked Grant from her line of vision. She sucked in a quick breath at the sight of him now. Though she was a tiny bit annoyed Grant hadn't listened to her about shopping on her own—but really, she hadn't expected him to—she was so relieved to see him she wanted to throw her arms around his neck. Instead she stood stock still, watching Paulos warily.

He had the look of a caged animal as he glanced back and forth between them.

And Grant appeared as if he was ready to strike. His eyes seemed a shade darker and his entire body was tensed in anticipation. He had that fighter stance thing going on. Though they were similar in height Grant was broader and Belle had no doubt he'd win in a fight with the other man.

Finally Paulos brushed past her instead of heading in Grant's direction. She stepped out of the way, keeping her basket up to block him as she watched him leave. Once he reached the end of the aisle and rounded the corner she breathed a sigh of relief.

Grant's strong hand settled on her shoulder, his fingers flexing as he gently massaged her shoulder. "Stay away from that guy, Belle."

She swiveled and looked up to face him. "You think I went looking for him?" The anger still burning inside her popped fiercely at his words. His *order*.

Immediately Grant's expression softened and he rubbed a hand over his face. "No. I just...I didn't even want to bring you here in the first place. Then to see and hear that asshole talking to you like that." His jaw clenched and that scary edge of anger she'd witnessed the first time he'd seen Paulos in her backyard crept into his eyes.

It suddenly registered that he was barely holding onto his control. If they hadn't been in a public place and if Belle hadn't been with him, something told her that Grant would have had more than words with Paulos.

Reaching out, she placed a gentle hand on Grant's forearm. "Come on. Let's get out of here so you can cook me dinner." She kept her voice light, teasing.

Grant chuckled under his breath, most of the tension dispelling from him, and nodded. "All right."

Linking her arm with his after he took the basket from her, she tried to ignore the butterflies that had taken up residence in her stomach whenever Grant was around. They'd spent almost every second with each other since her attack, but things were definitely platonic. Well, he looked at her with unmistakable lust when he thought she wasn't paying attention, but for the most part Grant was very contained. Too contained. She wanted to break that control, see what happened. Belle sighed, wondering if tonight maybe she'd get a repeat of the one kiss they'd shared, but knew if it was going to happen it would be up to her to make the first move.

* * *

Sitting in his van, he watched the pretty nurse step outside the supermarket with her arm loosely linked with Grant Caldwell's. They looked like such a happy couple it was nauseating. But it was also a miracle in a way. The good detective would never admit it, but this woman's presence in his life had brought him out of his pseudo-depression. He couldn't be completely sure, but it had seemed like Caldwell had been on the brink of falling into an abyss and now he was a changed man. For the last six months he'd lived like a hermit after leaving the hospital—only going to his physical therapy sessions and necessary places like the grocery store. Now he was acting like the man he'd been *before* the accident that ruined everything.

The only downside of the nurse's presence in Grant's life was that he was so focused on Belle that nothing else mattered. And that was absolutely unacceptable.

Steering out of his parking spot when Grant pulled away, he followed them at a safe distance until it was obvious they were returning to their neighborhood.

Grant kept Belle under lock and key ever since he'd almost drowned her. She was always safe. So untouchable.

Well, for now.

But she couldn't stay hidden forever and when the time was right, he'd strike. Turning down a side street, he cut through a local neighborhood as he headed toward the hospital where Belle worked. Using shortcuts, he was there in fifteen minutes.

After parking, he strode through the emergency room doors. He could have used the quieter, general welcome entrance, but he preferred this area of the hospital. It was busier and there was always the chance he'd find easy prey. A lot of victims of domestic abuse could be found here. Not that they were his preferred type, but he would make an exception if the situation was right.

Seeing mainly males and a few elderly people, he quickly dismissed anyone in the waiting room as a potential playmate. He had work to do today anyway. Some that pertained to his actual job and some that pertained to finding out more about Belle Manikas.

After going through security, one of the nurses buzzed him in past the main doors. Their security was usually tight but there was a different buzz in the air today. Everyone seemed edgy. He noticed the tense, stiff walk of the two security guys as they eyed him cautiously. He wasn't at the hospital often, just for on call situations, so he wasn't familiar with any of them.

The nurses, however, were a different story. He'd fucked a few of them, mainly just to pass his time in the last six months. Unfortunately none of them had gotten him really geared up. Enough to have sex, but that was it. None of them had that innocent quality he liked in his favorite playmates.

His shoes were silent as he strode toward the elevators. As he reached the closed doors, a blond annoyingly bubbly nurse sidled up next to him. The scent of her cloying perfume wrapped around him before he'd even looked down at her. His quick glance confirmed she was one of the last people he wanted to see, but maybe he could use her.

"Haven't seen you in a while," she said softly, her voice bordering on a whine. She didn't have that nasally tone he found nauseating in a woman, but everything about her grated on his nerves. From her fake blond hair to her giant fake tits.

They'd already fucked. He hadn't called. Why was she talking to him? He pasted on a practiced smile he knew came across as charming. In his business, he had to appear sincere. "I've been swamped with work." That much was actually true, but he set his own hours. He was in control of every aspect of his life. Just the way he wanted it.

She pushed out her bottom lip in a way he supposed she meant to be pouty, but was revolting. "So what are you doing here?"

"Just doing a follow up, but I was hoping to run into Belle Manikas while I was here." The first part of his statement was true. The second was a lie as he knew she wasn't working today. It was also guaranteed to piss off Nurse Nancy—God, what a stupid name—but he was almost counting on that.

Nancy's blue eyes narrowed venomously as the elevator doors dinged. "Why do you want to see her?"

He shrugged as he stepped inside. As he predicted, Nancy followed. When he didn't answer, she continued. "Well, you're out of luck. She's not working until this weekend and I know you *never* come in on weekends."

The elevator car stopped on the next floor where he promptly got out after murmuring a not-so-polite goodbye. He didn't care what Nancy thought of him, but at least he knew Belle's next work date. Now he could focus on finding out even more about her personal life. He'd done a little digging but not nearly enough. And the erotic dreams he'd been having about her weren't enough to satisfy him.

Even though he was incredibly patient, the more he thought about her, the hotter he became. Seeing that bruise on her face earlier made him smile at his handiwork. He'd been tempted to ease some of his tension in his van, but that would have been stupid and risky. He'd been careful for so long. Unlike many other criminals, he had no desire to ever get caught. He just wanted to keep playing his games. Resisting the urge to rub himself, he shifted uncomfortably and forced Belle's image to the back of his mind. Soon enough, a few bruises would be nothing compared to what he'd do to her. Then he'd have all the time in the world to relieve his tension using her body.

* * *

Belle sat at Grant's kitchen island, her legs crossed as she watched him cook. He was browning ground lamb in a frying pan for their gyros rather than baking it. She'd never had it this way, but she wasn't complaining. He'd been very creative in cooking for them the past couple nights and she was beginning to feel a little spoiled. She'd tried to help in the kitchen, but he'd refused to let her. At least she'd been able to help clean up—*once*. He was pretty insistent about taking care of the dishes too, which was incredibly sweet. She enjoyed him taking care of her, but she didn't like sitting around doing nothing. Of course after that run-in with Paulos, she didn't mind a little relaxing tonight. All she wanted to do was unwind and get to know Grant a whole lot better.

Preferably while they were both in his bed, naked.

She took another sip of her white wine as she eyed his broad, muscular back. He wore another long-sleeved shirt and even though she wanted to tell him to stop worrying about his scars, she respected him enough to let him make the choice in his own time. It bothered her that he didn't trust her enough to bare himself like that, but then she reminded herself that she'd only started wearing two-piece bathing suits at twenty.

Revealing her scar to the world had kind of been like a giant middle finger. She'd finally gotten to the point where she didn't care what anyone thought anymore. Of course her situation was different. Her scar was surgical and hidden beneath clothes most of the time. His face was scarred and she could understand Grant's hesitancy to bare himself. Even if she did think he was ridiculously sexy.

Feeling bold by her second glass of wine, she carefully set it down in front of her. "So…you've been pretty vague about your scars."

He went almost preternaturally still. His back went ramrod straight for a moment and it was as if all the air was sucked from the room. Just when she was about to take the question back, his shoulders loosened and he shrugged. It was definitely a touchy subject but she wanted to know everything that had brought him to this point in his life. How he'd become this man who for some reason seemed to think he needed to hide any part of himself from her. And that's exactly what he was doing with the long-sleeved shirts.

He cleared his throat and half-turned to look at her so the non-scarred side of his face was visible. "You know I was a cop." At her brief nod, he continued. "We'd received a tip about a cocaine lab about to be relocated within days. There wasn't time to wait to move on it. Long story short, we raided the place, I accidentally tripped a rigged bomb and..." He made a vague gesturing motion at himself with his hand.

Something about the quick way he'd told her the story didn't sit right. Last night he'd talked about his time in the Marines, then the couple years he'd spent on the SWAT team for the Miami PD before making detective. And he'd *accidentally* tripped something? "Grant, I'm not trying to sound like a jerk or anything, but I don't really see you making a mistake like that. Not with all your training. Did something else happen?" God, she really hoped she hadn't stepped in it with her question. Belle felt as if she was walking on those proverbial eggshells right now. There was just a note in his voice that had sounded off and some part of her wouldn't let this go.

Sighing softly, he added diced onions into the pan and started sprinkling everything with one of the three spice jars he had set out. "There was a kid involved. My focus was on him as I cleared one of the rooms. I was distracted and...when I stepped on the trigger I knew I was screwed. But I didn't want some innocent boy to pay the price. I used my body to shield him as best I could." Grant shrugged again but this time he didn't look at her.

A vise tightened around her heart, squeezing painfully. He never would have told her if she hadn't pushed. Right now she wanted to walk over to him and draw him into a big hug, but she held off. His body language was very clear. He did *not* want her touching him. Not to mention they weren't exactly at that point in their relationship anyway. Whatever their relationship was. "I'm so sorry for what happened to you, but that's incredibly brave. I'm not surprised you were thinking of someone else over yourself."

He grunted at her words, like she'd known he would. He'd been ridiculously protective of her ever since her attack in his pool. Almost as if he blamed himself for it. Grant had this way about him where he seemed to think he should be able to protect everyone.

She couldn't help asking one more thing. "What happened to the boy?"

Grant turned, a big smile on his face. "He was fine. A little bruised, but okay. I was knocked unconscious but I got to see him later. His name's Daniel. Came to visit me in the hospital and I found out a few days ago that he's being adopted into a good family. His mom was one of the women at the house and she gave up her rights.

Probably the only decent thing she's ever done for that kid," he murmured as he turned back to the stove.

Belle grinned at his back. He could be so closed off at times, but turn the conversation in the right direction and watch out. When Grant smiled, her entire world tipped off-kilter. Okay, it turned completely upside down. His expression and eyes softened when he smiled like that and her insides simply melted.

Fighting those dang butterflies bouncing around in her stomach, she froze at the sound of Grant's doorbell ringing. "Are you—"

Suddenly tense, he held up a finger to his lips, as if whoever was outside could actually hear her. She seriously doubted someone coming to harm either one of them would announce their presence so boldly. "I'll be right back." Then he was gone, lightning quick even with his limp.

Belle frowned and when she heard a female voice, her frown deepened even more. She started to slide off the chair but stopped when she heard Grant's laughter and the female voice getting closer. Feeling oddly out of sorts—Grant must have female friends, she reminded herself—she scooted back and picked up her glass of wine. Holding it helped steady her.

Until Grant appeared in the entryway with a tall, slender woman with long, dark hair, perfect tanned skin and toned arms and legs. She was definitely Hispanic—

Belle guessed maybe Cuban. Whoever she was, she was drop-dead gorgeous and in fantastic shape. She was also carrying a plate of what looked like homemade cookies. So she could bake too. *Great.*

For one moment, Belle experienced an insane surge of jealousy.

It dissipated the moment Grant said, "Belle, this is Elizabeth, my brother Porter's fiancé."

Relief grew inside Belle like an out of control vine. She slid off the chair and covered the few feet between them. "Hi, it's so nice to meet you."

The woman smiled warmly and held out a hand. "It's nice to meet you too. And please call me Lizzy."

Belle nodded and wondered why the woman was still grinning at her like the Cheshire cat. Lizzy looked back and forth between Grant and Belle and she realized the woman must think they were dating or something. Well, they definitely fell into the 'or something' category right now.

Unsure what to do, she motioned toward Grant's refrigerator. "Did you want some wine?"

Still smiling, the woman just shook her head. "No, I just wanted to drop these cookies off. Porter will be annoyed if I'm late for dinner."

Grant just grunted and took the plate, peeling back the cellophane as he carried it to the counter. Belle got a quick whiff of what were definitely chocolate chip cookies and her stomach rumbled. She'd be tearing into those soon.

"So, are you staying with Grant? Porter mentioned your attack...I'm sorry, I hope I'm not being rude. I just—"

"You were just sent over here as a spy for Porter, Harrison and likely Mara to find out more details about Belle," Grant said wryly.

Belle turned back to him, then to Lizzy and was surprised to see the woman's cheeks had flushed to a dark crimson. But she didn't deny the charge. His family was curious about her? She couldn't imagine why when Grant hadn't made a move or even given her a hint how he felt about her other than wanting friendship. Yeah, he was incredibly protective but that was just his personality type.

Feeling suddenly awkward, she took a step toward the entryway. "If you guys wouldn't mind excusing me for a moment, I'll be right back." She used the bathroom as an escape.

Sitting down on the closed toilet seat, she took a deep breath and tried to get her nerves under control. The spark of jealousy Belle had experienced before she'd known who Lizzy was had her insides shaking. What was wrong with her?

More importantly, she wondered what it meant that Lizzy had come over to basically spy on Grant. It clearly wasn't that common for him to have a woman around. Or she guessed so. Okay, hoped so. Well, even if there wasn't anything for Lizzy to report back to their family, Belle couldn't stand this feeling like she was in some weird limbo around Grant. She'd give him a few days, maybe a week, before making a move. Otherwise, she was bound to go crazy with all this pent up sexual frustration.

CHAPTER SIX

Belle hooked her purse across her body and fished her keys out before she'd even left the maternity ward. She put her keys into the front pocket of her blue scrubs then pressed the red button that opened the security doors.

Her first day back to work and almost a week after her harrowing attack and she was starting to feel semi-normal. She'd had dinner at Grant's every night this week and even stayed over a couple nights—in his *guest* room. He'd been very hands-off ever since last Saturday and while she appreciated his gentleness she was also getting a little frustrated.

Thanks to the insane security system Grant had had installed at her place, the nights she'd slept in her own home had been fairly peaceful. She'd woken up a few times from a nightmare but they were nothing a giant bowl of chocolate ice cream couldn't fix. She hadn't told her family or even her best friend about the attack. Instead she'd used moving in to her new home as an excuse to stay off the radar from everyone. Her mom had called once about Paulos Balis, wanting to know why the police had questioned him, but once she'd explained the situation her mom had gone freaking postal. Not on her, of course. And it had gotten her mom to back off with the phone calls this week which had been a miracle in itself. Belle figured her mom felt guilty for always trying to push Paulos on her.

A tiny part of her felt guilty for not telling her family what had happened but it would have created an avalanche of sympathy. Her family members would have descended on her house like locusts and it would have been even more stressful. She was incredibly grateful she had so many people who loved and cared about her, but she was tired of being treated like she was helpless. She'd tell them later once enough time had passed that they wouldn't worry.

Belle's sneakers squeaked against the tile as she made her way to the elevators. Her feet were more sore than usual, probably from when she'd kicked them against the pool wall, but at least they were mostly healed. Right now visions of wine, a hot bath and seeing Grant played in her head. She just wanted to get out of the hospital and the elevator was taking its sweet time. Under normal circumstances she liked to take the stairs, but after her attack she felt wary about even that. She hated that some deranged stranger had that kind of power over her life.

As the elevator dinged, her cell phone rang in her purse. When she saw Grant's number pop up, she couldn't help the smile that spread across her face.

"New boyfriend?" Brent, a male nurse she was friends with, asked as he stepped into the elevator with her.

Sliding the phone into her front pocket instead of answering, she could feel her cheeks heating up. Lord, was she that obvious? "Uh, not exactly." Okay, not at all. She wasn't sure what she and Grant were. They'd spent every night over the past week hanging out, talking and getting to know one another. And the man could certainly cook. He gave her all sorts of hot looks that told her he was interested in being more than friends, but he still didn't make a move. She'd already thrown herself at him once when she'd kissed him and she wasn't doing it again. She had *some* pride. The man was just so confusing.

Brent snorted and pressed the button for the ground floor. "I recognize that type of smile. You are so seeing someone."

Belle shrugged but couldn't fight her grin. Tonight she was going to ask Grant what was going on with them and what he wanted from her. The sexual frustration was likely to kill her otherwise.

She said a quick goodbye to Brent then grabbed her phone and pressed one of her speed dials—yeah, she knew she was in trouble now that he was on her speed dial.

Grant picked up on the first ring. "Hey, honey."

And he called her honey! The man was clearly trying to kill her with all these mixed signals. "Hey yourself. You off work?"

"Just pulled into the driveway. Want to come over for dinner?" His deep voice rolled over her like liquid sin.

She wanted to come over for a lot more than dinner. "Why don't we go out tonight? We can go to eat, maybe see a movie afterward?"

There was a moment of tense silence. Grant cleared his throat. "Ah..."

An invisible weight pressed down on her chest. "Are you ashamed to be seen with me?" She hated that her voice cracked on the last word. Warm, humid air rushed over her as the sliding glass doors opened up into the east parking lot. Nurses and doctors thankfully got front row parking.

"How can you even ask that?"

"You haven't asked me out once this week."

"You were just attacked and almost killed!" He sounded incredulous.

"That's not an answer."

She could practically see him rubbing a hand over his face the way he did when he was annoyed. "Belle, you're one of the funniest, most frustrating and yes, beautiful women I've ever met. There's no way I could ever be *ashamed* of being with you. I don't like the idea of taking you out in public until this lunatic is caught. I just want you safe."

"Oh." Her steps were silent as she weaved through the first row of cars. She was always vigilant about her surroundings but she still glanced around to make sure no one was following her.

"Have you…enjoyed the last week with me?" The hint of insecurity in his voice surprised her.

Her best friend would have told her to play coy, to hedge, but Belle couldn't do it. She couldn't play games with Grant. "Seeing you is the best part of my day. All I thought about at work today was hurrying home so I could spend time with you." Saying the words out loud was a little scary because yeah, there was no mistaking what she meant.

The silence seemed to stretch on forever and she could feel her face flaming when he didn't answer right away. She wished the ground would just open up and swallow her whole. She felt a presence behind her that hadn't been there before. A blur came at her from behind one of the cars.

"Belle—"

Her phone flew out of her hand as someone yanked on her purse strap, spinning her back around. Since it was across her body, her entire body jerked. She vaguely heard her phone clattering to the pavement.

Two arms wrapped around her from behind in a steely grip. After what had happened to her last week, a new kind of rage she'd never experienced before shot through her. *Hell no.* Using a move she'd learned in one of her self-defense classes, she slammed her head back and connected with something hard.

Her attacker's arms loosened as he cried out in pain. Without pause, she swiveled and turned with a raised elbow hoping to strike the guy again. As hard as she could, she slammed her elbow into the side of his head. It was a perfect shot and the only reason she got it in was because the guy had started to bend over from her first crack to his nose.

Pain shot up her arm from the sharp blow but the guy crumpled to the ground in a heap of dirty clothes, reeking of alcohol.

She started to run back toward the hospital when she spotted two familiar men sprinting toward her from a couple parking rows away. It was Travis and Vincent, the men who'd installed her security system. What was going on?

Travis spoke first. "Are you okay?"

"My elbow is throbbing but I'm fine... What on earth are you two doing here?"

The two men shot each other a look. Vincent's pale blue eyes against his coffee-colored skin were a sharp, beautiful contrast and the guilt shining there was palpable.

Before they could answer, she said, "Don't you dare lie to me. What's going on?"

When the guy on the ground started groaning and stirred, Travis sprung into action and handcuffed his wrists behind his back. "We uh, we've been hired to watch you," he muttered from his kneeling position, refusing to look at her.

So she narrowed her gaze at Vincent who blanched a little.

He cleared his throat. "Grant was worried about you going back to work today so—"

"He hired you to spy on me?" *And he hadn't told her?*

Travis jumped up at that. "No. He just wanted us to make sure you got home all right. That's it."

Belle knew she should be more focused on the guy who was likely a junkie or homeless man—or both—who had just attacked her, but he wasn't going anywhere and her temper had just lit on fire. Her entire life she'd been coddled by her family and she actually appreciated Grant's concern. Okay, more than appreciated it. She was damn grateful, but why all the secrecy? She wasn't a child to be kept in the dark. "How long was this supposed to go on for?"

Vincent shifted from foot to foot, looking around the parking lot. "You should talk to Grant about that...Hey, I see security." Before she could stop him, he was jogging toward a security guy driving a golf cart.

Her hands clenched into fists as it registered what Grant had done without telling her. Why would he keep something like that from her? She'd been able to take care of herself, but she could definitely appreciate the gesture. Just not all the secrecy.

Ignoring Travis, she searched the ground until she spotted her cell phone. By a miracle, the face of it wasn't damaged. Since Travis had pulled out his phone and was already calling the police she texted Grant, telling him what had happened and that if he knew what was good for him, he wouldn't meet her at the police station. She'd be home after she filled out a report and then they were definitely going to talk. She could handle over-protectiveness. The man was hardwired that way. But she couldn't deal with lies or half-truths. Not from a man she wanted a relationship with. It would put them on unequal footing and that was never healthy. Right now she didn't want to see him or even talk to him because she knew she'd lose her temper. Yep, letting her calm down was the best thing for both of them.

* * *

From the shadowed interior of his van he watched as the hospital security guy yanked the heroin addict he'd hired to attack Belle. Hire was a bit of a stretch. More like bribed with the promise of more drugs. The pretty nurse had certainly fought back, not that he'd expected any less.

Ever since his attack on her almost a week ago he'd done nothing but obsess about her, desperate for peeks of her. Originally she'd just been a means to an end. A way to target Grant Caldwell and bring the former detective back into their game. Ever since Caldwell's accident, the detective had been holed up in his house, avoiding everyone and everything.

Toying with someone in that state of self-pity and loathing was beneath him. But now it was obvious Caldwell was back on his feet and ready to play again. Killing the neighbor had seemed the perfect way to rope him back in. He'd wanted to do more than kill her of course, but when he'd come back to scope out both their houses and seen her swimming all alone, the opportunity had been too good to pass up.

Across the parking lot she crossed her arms protectively around her waist and leaned against her car as the security guy hauled the junkie to his feet. He'd briefly contemplated taking her from the hospital but she worked in one of the most secure areas—which meant that he couldn't take her from the inside. Belle took a step back from the junkie, scooting closer to the rear of the vehicle.

Holding him by his handcuffed wrists, the security guard guided the stumbling man to the golf cart where he forced him to sit. Then the same mohawked freak who'd shown up out of nowhere last week stood a foot from the handcuffed guy. He crossed his arms over his massive chest, making it clear that an attempt to flee would be monumentally stupid.

At least this evening hadn't been a total loss. He'd discovered his main concern had been correct. Belle had bodyguards. It would make taking her more difficult, but not impossible.

And take her he would. He just had to wait, watch and strike when she was most vulnerable. Even though he enjoyed being so close to her without her knowledge, it was time to leave. He eased his van out of the parking spot and drove toward one of the exits like he didn't have a care in the world.

CHAPTER SEVEN

Belle tapped her finger against Carlito Duarte's desk. She'd signed her statement and the crappy cup of coffee he'd given her wasn't much of an incentive to stick around. But he'd politely asked her to wait a moment while he'd gone somewhere with her statement.

Luckily the crime was pretty open and shut. Some junkie had tried to rob her. Idiot probably thought she was carrying hospital drugs or something. Or maybe he'd just wanted her money. Either way, one more addict was off the streets. Temporarily at least. After the events of last week, an attempted mugging was actually something she could emotionally deal with. Not that she was glad it had happened. But it was something she could wrap her mind around. Unlike the attack from before. An unwanted chill rolled through her at the thought but she locked the memory down tight. She just wanted to get this over with and go home.

As she started to glance around again, Carlito slid into his seat. His desk was one of about twenty in what he'd earlier called a bullpen. The giant room wasn't very impressive. Just incredibly bland. Desks, corkboards, men and women in police uniforms or suits milled around. Since she'd arrived it had gotten busier. Almost as if after dark it was expected for crime to get worse. From what she could see that was true. There had been a steady stream of officers leading people in handcuffs past her.

"How're you feeling?" he asked quietly, concern etched on his handsome face.

She knew he was only being nice but she was tired of people asking that. She was tired of being attacked. And she was really tired of the damn fear splintering through her. Her life had turned upside down ever since she'd moved out. Not that her move had anything to do with it, but still. She just wanted everything around her to calm down. "I'm good. Just tired and ready to go home." To see Grant. Being with him always made her feel safe and she wanted that badly tonight. Right after they talked about why he'd decided to keep her in the dark about her bodyguards.

He nodded but didn't make a move to get up. "I understand. Listen, the guy who attacked you tonight has a record. A long one. His DNA is in the system for...well, that doesn't matter. His DNA doesn't match the sample we took from your attacker last Saturday."

"I'm not surprised." Belle would never forget the strength behind her attacker's grip. Self-consciously she rubbed her jaw where she still sported a faded bruise from being punched. The guy who had attacked her today hadn't been very tall and he'd been fairly weak.

Carlito shifted uneasily in his seat and another healthy dose of panic settled inside her. "The man who attacked you—Justin—claims that a man hired him to attack you."

"*What?*" An icy fist clasped around her heart. That couldn't be right. But Carlito's expression was resolute.

The detective nodded, his face grim. "Justin's a junkie and I've dealt with him more times than I'd like to admit, but that's what he says. He's not getting a break by admitting this and he's still sticking to his story. I've got a sketch artist in with him right now, not that I think it'll do much good, but we have to try. He needs a fix and is pretty amped up."

Belle didn't know what to say. Someone had been hired to attack her. A shiver snaked down her spine at the insanity of the situation. She'd worked in the maternity ward at the hospital with the same people for years—and new mothers and fathers weren't exactly homicidal. She didn't frequent bars or clubs and usually spent the majority of her free time with her family or her best friend. Well, until recently when she'd been hanging out with Grant. She couldn't imagine having made an enemy that hated her so much he wanted to kill her.

"I know I asked you this last week, but is there anyone you can think of that would want to hurt you this bad?"

"*No.* This is…insane. I just…" Her voice caught in her throat so she shook her head, unsure how to continue.

Clearing his throat, Carlito stood. "All right. You've dealt with enough today. Do you have someone to drive you home?"

She snorted. "I think I can manage driving myself home." Though she had a feeling Travis and Vincent were still waiting for her in the lobby. Mainly because they'd told her they weren't going anywhere even when she'd insisted she'd be fine.

As they reached the door that opened up into the lobby of the three-story building, Carlito paused with his hand on the doorknob. His face slightly flushed underneath his flawless bronze skin. "Ah, normally I wouldn't do this but I wondered if you'd be interested in grabbing a drink sometime."

Belle blinked at him, sure she'd heard wrong. "Drinks? As in a date?"

His flush deepened and something told her that was unusual for this man. "Yeah."

Her eyes narrowed. "Aren't you friends with Grant?"

Surprise covered his expression. "He's one of my best friends."

"Then why are you asking me out?" Sure she and Grant weren't exactly dating...yet. But still, she was more than just friends with her sexy neighbor. She'd assumed Grant would have said something to his former partner about it.

"Oh, shit. Are you two dating? I asked him if there was anything between you two and he said you were just friends." Carlito rubbed a hand over his hair, looking extremely uncomfortable.

"He said we were just friends?" Hurt slammed into her like a semi-truck. On top of everything else that had happened today, this was the worst. Her hands clenched into balls. Not trusting her voice, she turned away from the detective. She opened the door and stepped out into the lobby even if it was rude. She didn't need an answer from him and she had nothing left to say to him anyway.

As she stepped into the lobby there were various clusters of people sitting in chairs. Including Travis, Vincent and Grant. She glared at Grant, whose indigo eyes just widened when he saw her. Without a word to any of them she grabbed her keys out of her purse and stalked for the glass doors. Striding across the parking lot, she tensed when Grant fell in line with her.

"You're pretty pissed at me, huh?" he asked quietly.

She didn't answer. Just pressed the keyfob on her keychain and jerked open the driver's side door. When he got in the passenger's side, she swiveled to face him. "You think I'm driving you home?"

"One of the guys is driving my car." He sighed heavily as she started the engine. "I should have told you I had them shadowing you, but I didn't want to freak you out. I figured better safe than sorry after what happened last week and—"

"You told Carlito we're just friends?" Damn, she did *not* know how to be subtle. She'd calmed down about the bodyguard thing because really, someone clearly wanted to hurt her and she couldn't get mad about Grant looking out for her. Yeah, she was annoyed he'd kept her in the dark, but she'd get over that too if it didn't become a habit. The thing with Carlito, however, pissed her off. Well, it actually hurt more than anything but anger was easier to latch onto.

"Uh…"

"If you're scrambling for an answer or a lie, don't bother. You told him we were just friends." Her voice was accusing. "Good to know."

"We *are* friends," he murmured.

Her fingers tightened around the wheel as she drove. "Do you kiss all your friends?" Of course it had been a week since that kiss so maybe there wasn't going to be a replay. No matter how mad she got at him, that thought was depressing.

"No. I didn't know what we were when he asked and hell, I still don't. I keep thinking you're going to wake up and see that you can do better than me." There was such a vulnerable note in his voice that it tore at her heart.

But not enough for her to back down. "I wish you could see yourself the way I do! You're compassionate, kind, gentle, funny, ridiculously protective—which is good and bad—and sexy. If you're so concerned about your perceived flaws and the way I look then maybe we should put the brakes on. If all you can focus on is my looks then—"

"Damn it, Belle! I don't see you like that. Okay, at first I noticed how gorgeous you are. I'd have been blind not to. Now that I've gotten to know you I see how much more there is to you. You're a smartass, incredibly thoughtful, and funny. And you have a temper."

She shot him a quick glance. "Having a temper is a good thing?"

His lips quirked up slightly, the action softening his entire face. "Oh yeah."

She swallowed hard and averted her gaze back to the road. Even though she wanted to say more she bit the words back. Earlier—right before she'd been accosted— she'd pretty much admitted to herself how she felt about Grant and she wasn't going to throw herself at him.

After a long, seemingly interminable moment, Grant spoke again. "I want more than friendship with you."

Belle let out a breath of relief she hadn't even realized she'd been holding. "Me too." As she pulled up to a stop-light, she risked another glance at him and almost wished she hadn't.

His eyes seemed even darker in the dim lighting of her car. They were also full of erotic promises. Despite the crap that had happened and the fear in the back of her mind about some lunatic trying to kill her, the heat-ed look Grant gave her *almost* made all that other stuff disappear.

Her gaze fell to his full lips and all sorts of wicked thoughts ran through her mind. Instinctively she mois-tened her lips with her tongue. Grant let out what she could only describe as a soft growl. Oh yeah, when they finally made it to the bedroom—a sharp horn blast made her jump.

The light had turned green and there was no telling how long she'd been staring at Grant like a lovesick moron. Keeping her hands firmly on the wheel and her eyes straight ahead, she didn't say another word. There would be time enough to talk later. Right now she didn't trust her voice or herself not to say something stupid. Like inviting him to take all her clothes off the instant they got back to her place.

The closer they got to their neighborhood she reached over and took one of his hands in hers. She needed to touch him. It grounded her in a way she didn't quite understand. When he laced his fingers through hers, she inwardly smiled. Tonight things were definitely going to change between them.

* * *

Grant entered his alarm code onto the numbered pad then slid the cover over it. He took a deep breath before stepping out of the small closet under the stairs. He'd left Belle waiting in the foyer while he set the alarm.

Mainly because he'd needed a few moments to get his shit together. Belle kept taking his breath away with her openness. Right now he wanted to kiss her so bad he ached for it. Well, he wanted to kiss and strip her naked. But that would mean he'd have to take off his clothes too.

He knew he had issues and was trying to come to terms with his own crap. It was just hard. If it had been another woman it wouldn't have mattered much. But Belle had the ability to destroy him. He was half in love with her and if she saw him naked, freaked over his scars and then rejected him…he didn't know if he could deal with that kind of rejection. Sighing, he headed down the short hallway to his foyer.

He froze in the entryway.

Belle's shoes, socks, scrubs—and bra and panties—were scattered from the front door all the way up his stairs. Holy shit. She was somewhere in his house *naked* and she was making sure he knew it. They'd come straight back to his place. He'd told her they'd get her clothes later and she hadn't cared.

She'd said she would just sleep in one of his shirts and that thought had been appealing so he hadn't argued.

The sound of running water upstairs jerked him into movement. Taking the stairs two at a time, he barely noticed his limp as he raced toward his bathroom and found himself hovering outside the stone and frosted glass wall of his custom made shower.

Only a foot separated them. He could see her silhouette under the water and she was singing a current hip hop song so off-key he couldn't hold back a laugh.

She paused and he watched as her hands fell from where she'd been massaging her head—likely with shampoo. "Took you long enough." Her voice was husky and sensual and he knew all he had to do was take a couple steps and see everything he'd been fantasizing about since the moment they'd met.

But his feet were leaden and he was unable to force his body into action.

Finally she started moving again, humming a familiar sounding tune and he realized she was giving him a choice. He could join her or not, but she wasn't going to push. Through the glass he could see her head fall back under water as she ran her hands through her hair. God, how he wanted to do that. To run his fingers through her tresses and grip the back of her head in a dominating grip.

"My entire back and left arm are scarred and it's not pretty," he blurted out.

"Okay." Belle continued humming and he realized he needed to get over himself.

If she rejected him then she wasn't who he'd thought. Would it destroy him? Oh yeah. But he'd never find out her reaction if he stood on the other side of the shower like a pussy. He'd been a Marine and a member of the Miami PD. He could do this.

Even though he was nervous he was still rock hard. Just being in the vicinity of Belle had that effect on him. But to know she was mere feet away from him, *naked*. Oh yeah, his erection wasn't going away any time soon.

Stripping off his clothes, he didn't look at himself in the mirror before stepping into the giant enclave. If he'd dared glance at himself he'd have chickened out.

Belle's back was to him, her face tilted up to the shower head as water rushed over her. Her dark hair was plastered against her back and her waist seemed even smaller because of the way her hips flared out. She had faint tan lines but thanks to her Mediterranean heritage her skin was a gorgeous olive tone. Even her backside was a pale brown, only a shade lighter than the rest of her body.

A body he wanted to run his hands and mouth all over. She was petite but surprisingly curvy. His entire body tensed as he imagined grasping her hips as she rode his cock.

Unable to stop himself, he stepped forward and skimmed his hands along her sides, flexing his fingers on her soft skin. She paused for all of a second before turning to face him. Her green eyes were wide and nervous, but the spark of desire in her expression nearly floored him. Forcing himself to keep his gaze on her face he took a step forward, his erection pressing firmly against her belly.

Heat flashed in those green depths. When she slid her hands up his chest and tentatively rested her fingers on his shoulders, he stilled and took a small step back.

"Before we take this any further I want you to see what you're getting." His voice was raspy and uneven. The primal part of his brain told him to just take what she was offering, but he couldn't do that to her. He wanted her walking into this with eyes wide open. She was so damn honest about everything, he needed to do this.

With all his muscles tensing, he turned around. Even though he couldn't see her, he closed his eyes, fighting his natural instinct to cover himself.

Gentle hands slid along his shoulders, then down his back in an almost reverent stroke. He didn't have feeling in the scarred areas, but there were a few patches along his back that had been spared. When he felt Belle's soft lips press feather light kisses down some of the scar-free areas on his spine, he shuddered. Even though he couldn't feel all of her kisses, he knew she was kissing the entirety of his back. Something deep inside him, something primal he didn't even know existed, flared to life and he realized that Belle was the one for him. He should have been terrified, but a rightness settled in his gut at the knowledge.

Not only was she not bothered by his scars, but she was obviously trying to make him as comfortable as possible.

Needing to touch her, he turned, taking in her entire body this time. Her breasts were full, round and bigger than he'd realized even though he'd seen her in a bathing suit. Her nipples were a dark brown, contrasting perfectly against her olive skin. He ached to hold, stroke and kiss all over her until she was writhing against his mouth and hands.

But he wanted to see all of her first.

The scar on her chest he'd only gotten a peek at before was almost twelve inches long. Over dinner one night she'd explained that she'd needed to have heart valve replacement surgery more than once when she was younger. The medical community had come a long way since then, but less invasive methods hadn't been available when she'd been ten and needed open heart surgery. Even the thought of her going through something like that shook him to his core. She might appear fragile, but she was clearly a survivor and he loved that about her. After everything she'd been through the past week, she was a rock. That was damn sexy.

His fingers flexed on her hips as he continued his perusal. The soft thatch of dark hair between her legs was perfectly trimmed. His hips rolled against hers as his cock jerked at the sight. Yeah, his body was ahead of his brain. He wanted inside her so bad he practically shook with the need.

Even though his body was shouting at him to take her hard and fast, he slowly bent to kiss her. He'd planned to take things gradually. To ease her into this. Give her all the foreplay she deserved. To stroke her to orgasm at least once before he entered her.

But once their lips touched, Belle's kisses were frantic and needy. She grabbed his shoulders and lifted herself up, wrapping her legs around him. Damn, he loved how bold she was. When she wanted something she just went for it.

Pressing her against the wall, he covered her mouth, pushing, teasing with his tongue and taking everything she'd give him. Her tongue danced against his with bold, demanding strokes. Each time he met her caresses, she arched her back, pressing her full breasts against him.

The feel of her hard nipples rubbing against his chest was almost enough to short circuit his brain. Cupping one in his callous-roughened hand, he inwardly smiled when she shuddered and tightened her thighs around him.

It wouldn't take much to shift their bodies so he could push deep into her, but he held off. Somehow he tore his mouth from hers and bent until he sucked one of her nipples into his mouth. Using his teeth, he gently tugged.

Belle gasped and moaned, letting out such hot sounds he barely restrained himself from just taking her. First she needed to climax. Hell, he needed her to. Giving her pleasure felt like the most important thing at the moment.

As he flicked over her nipple, alternating between using his teeth and tongue, he cupped her mound. Instead of teasing, he slid two fingers inside her in one swift stroke. Her inner walls clenched and she lifted up off of the wall, clinging to him.

He smiled against her breast as she clutched his shoulders and back, using his body instead of the wall for support.

"Yes, yes," she moaned.

As he began moving his fingers in and out of her she grinded against his hand with complete abandon. He placed his thumb right over her clit, rubbing it with an intense pressure he hoped would bring her to a hard climax. With each stroke her slick sheath tightened around him and all he could imagine was sliding into her wetness. Except...he needed a condom.

Grant wanted to groan aloud as he realized they'd have to wait. But that didn't mean he couldn't bring her all the pleasure she deserved in the meantime.

Continuing with a steady rhythm of his fingers and thumb, he pulled his head back from her breast as an orgasm tore through her. Belle's head fell back as she shouted his name. Her dark, wet hair fell around her face and chest in thick wet strips as she closed her eyes, completely lost in bliss.

As the orgasm ebbed, her lids fluttered open. She stared at him, blinking a few times until a soft smile played across her slightly swollen lips. "That was...wow," she said, clenching around his fingers which were still buried inside her.

Slowly, he withdrew from her though he hated doing it. When she shifted her body up his, he realized what she was doing and stilled her with a firm grip on her waist.

Her pretty mouth pulled into a thin line. "Why are you stopping?" she whispered, a touch of hurt in her voice.

Sighing, he laid his forehead against hers. Water splashed them, ricocheting off the walls and floor. He swallowed once. "I don't have any condoms."

"Crap, I wasn't even thinking," she murmured. Belle was silent for a long moment after that, and her next words surprised the hell out of him. "I'm on the pill, but I haven't been with anyone in five years. I'm clean and healthy."

The words seemed to reverberate off the walls as he realized he could sink into her body with no barriers. It was hard to fathom that she hadn't been with anyone in so long but he believed her. "I was tested almost a year ago and...I haven't been with anyone since then either. But if you want to wait I understand. I don't want—"

Belle wrenched her body up and slid over his cock so fast he almost climaxed from the shock of feeling that tightness encasing him. Damn she was snug. He pushed out a long breath and slid a hand through her dark hair, holding the back of her head and steadying her. Hell, steadying himself.

She cupped the scarred side of his face and watched him with a slight smile as she clenched around his cock. The feel of her inner walls tightening on his hard length was akin to electric shocks shuddering through his body.

He felt the sensation slamming into all his nerve endings.

Her mouth parted slightly, but she didn't make a move to kiss him. He didn't make a move to either. Just continued moving his hips against hers, savoring her warmth, the sense of rightness he felt with her.

"Faster," she whispered, the need in her voice taking him off guard.

With a soft growl he pulled back and slammed into her. The abrupt action had her crying out. He followed suit, burying his face against her neck as he lost himself inside her.

He lost all track of time and their surroundings as he continued pushing inside her until unparalleled pleasure slammed into him. He cried out against her neck as she clutched his shoulders, digging her nails in.

As he emptied himself inside her in hard strokes, he realized she was climaxing again too. Her cries intermingled with his until she sagged against him, her entire body limp. His own legs were barely holding them up.

Even though he wanted to hold her forever, he eased her down, placing her on her feet. Grabbing his washcloth he squeezed a little body wash onto it and gently swiped between her legs. As he did, she feathered kisses across his chest, making his heart swell with a foreign emotion he was scared to define even though he knew exactly what it was.

CHAPTER EIGHT

Belle opened her eyes to find Grant watching her intently. Muted light seeped in from the curtain-covered window across from his bed, illuminating his massive, muscular form. Her entire body pulsed and tingled as she remembered last night in his shower—and then hours later in his bed he'd woken her again. She glanced up at the wall clock by the window. It was only five in the morning. She had hours until she needed to be at work. They could certainly do a lot in that time frame.

Stretched out next to her, the lower half of Grant's body was covered by the tangled mess of his comforter, but she could see his arousal quite clearly. His erection pushed insistently against the covers as if it was trying to break free. She, on the other hand, was completely bare, having kicked the covers off sometime during the night. Normally she slept in pajamas but she could get used to the freeing sensation. The coolness from the running air conditioner brushed over her skin, but it did nothing to douse the heat burning through her at Grant's hungry look. He reached out and laid a callused hand on her waist, gently stroking upward until he *almost* cupped her breast.

Heat bloomed between her legs and she instinctively clenched them together.

His eyes were almost a midnight blue in the shadowy room and she had no doubt he wanted her again. Which was good because she hadn't gotten nearly enough of him last night.

Reaching out, she trailed her fingers down his chest until she dipped beneath the covers and grasped his hard length. She smiled, liking that he was already hard for her. His sucked in a breath and the fingers on her hip tightened possessively, making her smile even more.

"I've been waiting half an hour for you to wake up." His voice was uneven and raspy.

"Is that right?" she murmured.

He just groaned when she stroked him once, twice, three times. Making such a dominant, sexy man shudder made her feel powerful in a way she hadn't realized she could easily start to crave. Pulling her hand back, she pushed at his chest until he was on his back.

Belle had only had one lover—and that term was a bit of a stretch—when she was in college. The few times she'd had sex before Grant had been perfectly pleasant. And perfectly forgettable. After that experience she'd never had the urge to repeat it. Not with her full load of classes at school and then her full time job at the hospital. Why bother with something that didn't give a worthwhile reward? Of course her feelings on that had changed practically the moment she'd met Grant.

He just exuded a kind of power and sex appeal she could barely explain to herself. All he had to do was look at her and heat bloomed between her legs. She felt a little crazy for the reaction he brought out in her, but she wouldn't change it for anything.

Shoving the covers off, she quickly straddled him. She loved how broad and muscular he was everywhere. For a moment she was overwhelmed, wondering where she should start kissing him. His stomach muscles clenched when she lifted up on her knees, brushing her wet sheath across his hard length.

Teasing him was too much fun even if it was torturous to her own sanity. She was already slick with wanting him.

As she slid her hands up his body, bending forward until her breasts brushed against his chest, his fists tightened on her waist. She knew he wanted to just lift her and impale her on him but he held back. She could feel the bare restraint humming through him. The fact that he was holding back was incredibly hot. But it only made her want to tease him even more.

She started feathering kisses along his collarbone, nipping with her teeth then following up with strokes of her tongue. His hips kept jerking upward, his cock nudging her entrance insistently.

As if she didn't know what he wanted.

Smiling against his skin, she couldn't hold back a giggle. That's when she found herself flat on her back, the air rushing from her lungs.

Grant's eyes narrowed. "You're enjoying teasing me," he growled, a bite of neediness in his voice.

"Of course I am." She stretched her arms above her head, grasping onto the headboard. Daring him to take over. The action pushed her breasts out and drew his gaze to them, just like she wanted. He'd already proved he had a very talented mouth and she wanted it on her body now.

Immediately his head dipped and he was licking and sucking. He feasted on her like he was a starving man. Her inner walls clenched with the need to be filled by him until the absence was almost painful. She squeezed her legs around him and lifted her hips, trying to entice him. No such luck.

Each time he stroked one of her hard nipples, she felt the sensation shoot straight between her legs. The tingling in her clit was almost unbearable. "Now who's the one teasing?" she managed to gasp out.

He chuckled against her breast, the sound rolling through her entire body. Combined with his stubble rubbing against her, her breasts felt over sensitized. Lifting her hips against his again she figured he'd take the hint this time, but he surprised her by grasping her waist and flipping her onto her knees.

Looking at him over her shoulder, she watched in fascination as he stared at her body in an almost reverent way. Like she was some sort of pagan offering. That thought was wildly erotic. Of course only if she was being offered up for him to feast on. A shudder ripped through her as images of their intertwined bodies danced in her mind.

His chest rose and fell, the harshness of his breathing filling the room. He slowly ran a callused hand down the length of her spine before settling on her backside. Then he trailed a finger down her crease. She tensed, wondering what he was doing, but when he continued until he pushed into her wet sheath, she let out a low moan.

Belle wanted a lot more than his finger and she didn't want slow right now. Before she could tell him exactly what she needed, he removed his finger. He grasped her, his hands flexing on her hips in a tight, dominating grip and he thrust into her.

She was a little sore from last night but not enough to stop. When he'd woken her during the night he'd slowly made love to her, but she felt almost frantic right now.

Even though she'd been able to defend herself from that attacker yesterday she'd been scared out of her mind. And even though she'd told Grant to stay away, he hadn't. He'd come to the police station knowing he'd face her anger. He'd been there for her. The man could be pushy and a little overbearing but with him she found she didn't mind. He listened when it really mattered and right now he was listening to what her body wanted.

It amazed her how he'd learned what she liked so quickly. When she tightened her grip on the headboard to steady herself, one of his hands slid from her hip to her mound. He moved his finger over her clit in bold strokes. Normally when she touched herself it was with steady soft caresses. His rougher touch should have been too much. Hell, it almost was, but his teasing pushed her over the edge so quickly she didn't realize she'd been so close to climax.

Her back arched as her inner walls rippled around Grant's hard length. Her orgasm seemed to go on forever, pulsing around him until he was coming with her.

"Belle," he gasped out, the need in his voice punching through her.

The feel of his heat inside her as he climaxed was even more arousing. As he eventually stilled behind her, she slowly eased forward and twisted around so she was facing him.

Needing to hold him, she wrapped her arms around him and buried her face in his neck until limp and exhausted, she finally fell back against the mattress. The bed was soft, inviting and she could barely keep her eyes open as she felt Grant stretch out next to her.

He tugged her until her back tucked against his torso, but she still didn't open her eyes. She'd completely fallen for Grant and part of her wanted to tell him. But she was nervous of how he'd react. She was scared he'd reject the truth of her feelings, try to tell her she didn't care for him as much as she did. Or worse, maybe he'd just completely push her away. Sighing, she cuddled deeper against him. She had time to worry about that stuff later. Now she just wanted a few more hours of sleep before she had to get up for work.

* * *

Belle pulled her hair back into a ponytail before glancing at herself one last time in the mirror. She'd left Grant's place half an hour ago to get ready for work even though she could have stayed in bed with him all day. She wanted to stop and pick up coffee on the way to the hospital. She had a solid twelve hour shift ahead of her and desperately needed a caffeine fix.

As she hooked her purse over her shoulder, her doorbell rang. Wondering who it was—and hoping it was Grant—she hurried downstairs. She peeked through the peephole and saw a man wearing a baseball cap with the name of the furniture store she'd ordered her new guest bed set from.

She disabled the alarm but instead of answering right away, she looked out the window of her living room just to make sure it wasn't some guy in a stolen uniform. Sure enough, a big delivery truck with the same company name emblazoned on the side of it was in her driveway. Feeling a little foolish—and cursing her unknown stalker for this constant fear that lived inside her now—she called through the door. "What are you delivering?"

She watched him through the peephole. He looked down at a notepad. "Ah, says here I'm delivering the 3-piece Oasis Oak bedroom set."

Relief coursed through her as she opened the door. She smiled and held the door open. "I totally forgot you were coming this morning. I'm so glad I haven't left for work yet."

The man adjusted his cap and smiled at her, but something about him was off. A thread of unease slid down her spine, chilling her veins. His dark brown eyes seemed almost devoid of emotion and his smile definitely didn't reach his eyes. "I'm glad you haven't left either."

That's when she saw the stun gun in his hand.

Terror forked through her, splintering out like jagged lightning to all her nerve endings. She turned to run, to hit the distress button on her alarm keypad, but his arm shot out and the taser connected with her neck.

Pain like she'd never known blasted through her. Paralyzed from the electrical voltage, she fell to her knees then onto her face. Her cheek throbbed where she'd fallen but it was almost dull compared to the tiny knives of agony shredding her nerves. All her muscles spasmed out of control but she couldn't move. That alone was terrifying—then to see the man bending over her but not being able to do anything chilled her bone deep.

Blinking through tears, she opened her mouth and tried to scream but only a croak of nothingness escaped. A syringe flashed in her attacker's hand and she was helpless to avoid it as he plunged it into her neck. The sting was fleeting.

She struggled to hold on to consciousness, just like she'd done in the pool, but a dark wave of blackness swept over her, tugging her under until she had no choice but to stop fighting it.

* * *

Grant stepped out onto his front porch, phone in hand. He'd called Belle once, wanting to see her before she left for work. She'd told him she wanted to give him a kiss goodbye and even though it made him feel like a stupid teenager, he was excited at the thought. After last night he figured he should be somewhat sated, but no such luck. He was apparently greedy because the more he touched her, the more he wanted her.

When he saw a furniture delivery truck in her driveway he headed over, figuring he could help. It was Saturday and even though Belle had to work, it was his day off. He could set up the furniture for her while she was gone if it wasn't included in her delivery fee.

He rang the doorbell but no one answered. Frowning and trying to ignore the instinctive increase in his heart rate, he tried the handle. The door swung open and he immediately spotted her keys on the tiled entryway.

Fuck. "Belle!" Even though the most primitive part of him *knew* she wouldn't answer, he called out her name.

When he didn't get an answer he crept down the hallway until he made it to the kitchen.

Empty.

Grabbing a knife so he'd have a weapon, he quickly raced through the house checking each room. An eerie silence had descended. It had the kind of emptiness that made him positive he was alone, but he had to check. Had to make sure she wasn't...no, he couldn't even think the word.

Belle was alive. She just had to be.

There was an impossible pressure on his chest, making it difficult to breathe but he pushed past it. Losing his shit right now would only hurt Belle and he'd be damned if that happened.

Hurrying back outside, he raced to the delivery truck. Standing on the running board of the big vehicle, he peered in the driver's side window and his heart caught in his throat.

A man wearing a white undershirt and boxers had his hands secured behind his back, his feet also bound and a gag in his mouth. He was stretched out on the bench seat, his body half falling into the passenger side floorboards. Grant jerked the door open. The restrained man grunted and started wriggling around, which only made him fall completely onto the floorboards.

"I'm going to cut your bindings free. Don't move." When the guy stilled, Grant made quick work of the flex-cuffs on his wrists and ankles.

The man turned over and pushed up onto the passenger seat. While the Hispanic man with the dark hair was pulling the gag free, Grant didn't bother with niceties. He needed to find out where Belle was. "What happened? Did you see where he took the woman?"

The driver rubbed his wrists as he shook his head. "Some guy hit me with a stun gun. I was still conscious even if I couldn't move when he was stripping me and I thought he'd kill me, but..." The man shrugged jerkily, obviously shaken.

"Did he say anything else?"

"Just that if I didn't struggle he wouldn't kill me." He snorted. "I couldn't move anyway."

"You got a phone?" When he nodded, Grant said, "Good. Call the cops. Tell them what happened and give them this address."

"Okay. What are you doing, man?" he called after him, but Grant was already sprinting back to his house as fast as he could go, his limp barely slowing him down.

His determination to find Belle overrode everything else. As he grabbed his cell out of his pocket, it rang. When he saw Belle's number on the caller ID, all the air sucked from his lungs. His fingers shook as he pressed the receive button. "Hello?"

"Your little neighbor is quite beautiful, isn't she?" a male voice he didn't recognize asked.

"Where the hell is she?" Asking was futile but he did anyway.

"Did you really think I would let you walk away? Let you quit playing our game?" There was raw anger in the man's questions.

Fighting panic, Grant continued toward his house as he asked, "What are you talking about?"

The caller snarled a curse. "I'm talking about Abigail Moore, Ruth Bailey, Lisa Flores and Virginia Palmer."

Grant's entire body chilled, his palms turning clammy as he shut his front door behind him. Before he'd been in his accident he and Carlito had been hunting a serial rapist/killer in the greater Miami area. He sure as hell hadn't forgotten the case but according to his former partner, there hadn't been any new victims in the last six months. Thank God for that. They'd both wondered if the killer had moved on to a new hunting ground or had possibly been arrested for a different crime.

The killer hadn't left DNA behind at any of the scenes so they hadn't been able to cross-reference anything with either CODIS or IAFIS. Of course this could be a copycat or just a lunatic off the street. Though he doubted it. Belle hadn't been worried about her family's friend Paulos Balis, but Grant had assigned someone from Red Stone to watch the guy. Unless he'd slipped his watcher Grant could eliminate him as the man behind Belle's kidnapping.

"What do you know about those women? Read about them in the newspaper?" Grant needed to know for sure who he was talking to. He hurried up the stairs while he kept the guy on the line.

"I remember how it felt to carve my initials into their shoulders. To slowly slice up their perfect bodies while they screamed in agony. I also look at their undergarments every day. I keep them tacked up in my...workshop."

Grant forced himself to keep moving as he digested this monster's words. A slow rage was building inside him like a volcano, but if he let it take over he'd be no good to Belle. Through his anger and helplessness, he reminded himself of that.

He and Carlito had always wondered what the two letters carved into the victim's back left shoulder meant and they'd never found a similar MO in any law enforcement databases so there had been nothing to cross-reference. They'd also never mentioned that the killer took trophies from his victims but this guy knew.

And he had Belle.

Grant's hand fisted around the SIG he'd pulled from his nightstand, wishing he could empty it into this guy's chest right then. The thought of Belle at the mercy of such a monster caused a red haze to blind Grant for a moment. "What do you want from me?"

"You to invest time in our game again. We stop playing when *I* say we stop!" His heated words caused Grant to still.

He needed to keep his cool and to keep this guy talking. If he was on the phone, he wasn't hurting Belle. "Okay, I'm listening and I'm ready to play again."

"Good. After I'm finished with your neighbor, I'll call you." His voice was icy calm. Then he hung up.

"No!" Grant shouted but it was too late. Adrenaline pumped through him overtime as he called Harrison. He had limited clues and no idea where this guy took his victims. They'd always been dumped in public places before. Days after they'd been killed. Well, the last three had been dumped that way. The first victim had been killed years ago and no one had made the connection to the recent victims until Grant.

His brother answered on the second ring. "Yeah?" Harrison barked, sounding tired and agitated.

"Someone's taken Belle. From that serial rapist case I worked before my accident. He's smart and he just called me from her phone. I think he's smart enough to take out her phone battery so I can't track her but—"

"I'm on it. Stay on the line." He heard Harrison cursing then having a conversation with someone.

Grant guessed his brother had called one of their computer specialists to track Belle using the extra tracking device he'd placed in her phone. He knew it was underhanded, but he hadn't done it to spy on her. Hell, he couldn't just track her from his own computer. This device was linked to a private, intra-office system at Red Stone. They rarely used these types of devices and only for special dignitaries when they were worried about kidnappings. Grant had put one in Belle's phone for her protection and had planned to tell her once they'd found her stalker. Well, his stalker as it turned out. Now he could only hope the damn thing worked.

Moments later Harrison was back on the line. He rattled off coordinates which turned out to be a residential address only ten minutes from where Grant lived. He could hear sirens in the background and knew the cops were on the way to check out the scene of Belle's kidnapping and that delivery driver's assault. He needed to be gone before that happened because he wasn't waiting for anyone to save Belle. Plus he couldn't risk them trying to haul him down for questioning.

"Call Carlito and relay everything to him. Tell him to meet me there but no fucking sirens," Grant ordered as he palmed his car keys. He wasn't calling anyone else about this or wasting any more time talking. He could barely get the order out to his brother.

"Done. I'll also call Porter. We'll be there as soon as we can."

Grant wanted to tell him and his brother to stay the hell away. He could handle this and he didn't want more of his family involved with someone clearly insane, but he didn't bother. His brother wouldn't listen, just as Grant wouldn't if placed in the same situation. After he entered the address into his GPS system he tore out of his driveway. When he passed a black and white with its lights and siren on, he didn't even pause.

Saving Belle was the only thing that mattered. She'd just come into his life and there was no way in hell he could lose her. He loved her, even if he hadn't been able to admit it to himself earlier. She was everything he'd never realized he needed in life and he *would* save her no matter what it took.

CHAPTER NINE

Belle tried to open her eyes but it felt like something was weighing them down. Drugs...she'd been drugged with something. She remembered opening her front door to a delivery guy. No, obviously not a delivery guy but she couldn't dwell on that now. Dread settled on her chest, pushing at her until she wanted to curl into a ball and hide. But she couldn't move. Whatever he'd injected her with was still working.

Struggling, she forced her eyes open. They only opened a sliver but she could see wood beams high above her. So she was indoors. As she moved her head to the left a dull pain spread through her skull. She didn't react to drugs well so she imagined she'd have the headache from hell now that whatever she'd been injected with was wearing off.

Of course that was the least of her worries considering someone had taken her from her home. Blinking a few times, she managed to focus on what looked like a workbench. There was a long, wicked looking knife and some other metal tools she didn't recognize splayed out. Above it were pictures of pretty, smiling women. There were four of them. All had dark hair but they looked like different ethnicities. One was Hispanic, another had Native American roots, one white and the last Belle wasn't sure. She had beautiful café au lait colored skin and her dark brown hair was pulled up into a sleek chignon.

Belle began to shake as she realized why the women looked familiar. The pictures were all cut out from newspapers. They were pictures of the four women who had been kidnapped, tortured, raped and killed last year. No...one of them had been killed years ago but she'd been linked to the other three killings if Belle remembered right. They'd been all over the headlines for months until one day the killings just stopped. She'd actually forgotten about it once the media coverage died down.

Panic burst inside her and she tried to sit up, but she couldn't get her muscles to function. Looking down she realized she'd been strapped down on a metal table. Her ankles were secured with metal clamps, though there was a soft material in between the restraints and her skin. It struck her as odd but the terror splintering through her overrode almost all her rational thoughts.

Her wrists were strapped down parallel to her hips. They'd been secured in the same fashion as her ankles. For a moment she contemplated calling out for help but from her limited view it looked as if she was in a small workshop. No windows, only walls and a door. Something deep inside her told her that shouting would do no good. Whoever had taken her had left her alone and he hadn't covered her mouth. Which meant he didn't care if she screamed. Or maybe he planned on her doing just that to alert him she was awake.

She hoped her captor didn't know she was awake yet. *She needed to get free.* Pulling and thrashing she tried to tug her wrists or ankles free. It was no use. The restraints were secure and all she accomplished was tiring herself out.

Tears welled up in her eyes. She tried to fight them, to keep her panic at bay but it was no use. They spilled down her cheeks and the sides of her face as she managed to bite back a sob. She was terrified of making a noise and alerting the man who'd taken her that she was awake.

When she heard the door handle rattling and then the sound of a lock sliding free she took in a deep breath and let out an ear-splitting scream the moment the door opened. If this place was sound-proofed—and if this guy had managed to torture and kill four women already she had to assume it was—she had to try to alert someone while the door was open.

The same tall man who'd been posing as a furniture delivery guy opened the door and slammed it with a snarl. "I see you're awake."

Even though she was still dressed, the way he looked at her made her feel naked and exposed. She fought a shudder but lost. She was terrified out of her mind. No sense denying it.

Keeping his dark gaze on hers, the man still wearing the simple uniformed collared-shirt from earlier slowly walked toward her like the predator he was. He stopped right next to her head, staring down at her with those dead-looking eyes.

He smiled as he stroked a finger down her cheek. Blanching, she jerked her head in the other direction but he just chuckled. "I see why Detective Caldwell fell for you," he murmured, his voice soft despite the underlying deadly edge.

Grant? What did this guy know about him? Sensing he wanted her to respond, she kept her mouth shut.

"Nothing to say to that?" he snapped, clearly annoyed with her.

What the hell *could* she say? A light sheen of sweat covered her face and arms despite the chill of the room. She could practically taste the bitterness of her own fear in her mouth and it was disgusting. Darting her gaze around, she continued to look for any weakness in the room but the only opening was the now closed and locked door. Not to mention she was still tightly secured.

As if he read her mind, her captor chuckled. "There's no escape for you. I soundproofed this shed myself. I do all my *work* right behind my house, close to where I live, eat and sleep. If only the neighbors knew what I did in here." He laughed again, the sound reverberating off the small room and making her sick to her stomach.

Nausea roiled inside her and she was grateful she hadn't had a chance to eat breakfast or even drink coffee. If she had, she'd be puking it up right now. Taking a deep breath she decided to talk. "You took me because of Grant?"

"She speaks," he said as he picked up a long, gleaming knife that had clearly been sharpened recently.

God, maybe she would be sick. She swallowed hard, trying to keep the bile down. Tensing, her instinct was to start thrashing around. Somehow she managed to stay still, knowing it wouldn't do any good. Her hands balled into fists and her toes curled as she locked all her muscles.

Grabbing the collar of her sea blue hospital uniform, he flicked the knife down the middle of it, splitting her shirt completely open. Belle tried to shrink away from his stare as if she could somehow make herself invisible or at least smaller, but there was nowhere for her to go.

Swallowing hard, she took another deep breath, ready to scream again when he just laughed and bent down until their faces were inches apart.

His breath was hot on her cheek. "Scream all you want. No one will hear you." He continued laughing, the sound hollow as he turned back to the table.

He wanted her to scream. The realization slammed into her stomach with the intensity of a two by four. She'd hold off as long as she could if only to deny him satisfaction. But judging from the tools on the workbench and what little details the police had released to the media about the former victims, she knew she would end up screaming. As a nurse, she understood the body and mind could only take so much until they broke. But she'd be as strong as she could for as long as possible.

Her entire body turned icy as she tried to steel herself against what he'd do to her. Enough horrific images flashed in her mind—God, why did she have to be so morbid—that she began struggling to breathe when she noticed the door handle slowly turning.

Maybe it was her imagination, her mind seeing what it wanted to, but she blinked when she saw that it was *definitely* moving. A tiny gasp escaped and her captor looked over at her, his eyes narrowing.

"So why did you target Grant? Clearly this isn't about me." She was proud that her voice only shook a little when she spoke. She had to do everything she could to distract him even if it meant keeping his focus on her.

Turning his full attention on her, knife still in hand, he stepped closer to where she was stretched out. His dark eyes roved over her body and she wanted to disappear. As he brought the knife down toward her she flinched, expecting him to cut or stab her. Instead, he sliced the middle of her bra, letting it fall open. Vaguely she wondered why he'd even bothered leaving her clothes on but figured this was all part of his sick, twisted game. He liked to witness the terror on his victim's faces as he stripped them. Realizing that, she tried to keep her face a mask but knew she was failing.

The room was freezing and her nipples hardened under the chilly air. The unstoppable reaction made her cringe especially when his gaze landed on her breasts. He rubbed his thumb over one nipple, watching her face as he did. She wanted to puke at the physical contact, but didn't respond. Just tightened her jaw until it hurt so bad her head started to ache.

His hand dropped as he took a step down her body. "Detective Caldwell is intelligent. He discovered Ruth Bailey, my second victim in Miami. And *he* is the one who made the connection between her and Abigail Moore."

Abigail Moore. Belle remembered part of the story, but she hadn't followed the news that closely. Moore had been killed five years ago. An unsolved, grisly rape and murder. The other three murders had been spread out exactly one month apart. Out of the corner of Belle's eye she could see the door slowly opening. Hope leaped in her chest. *Keep him talking*, she ordered herself. "I don't really follow the news but you killed her years before the other three murders, right? Why did you wait so long in between? And why stop?" If she could get him to start talking about himself she hoped it would distract him even more.

He dragged the dull edge of the blade along her scar. The feel of the cold metal and her exposure to his lustful gaze made her flinch. She tried so hard to remain immobile, to compartmentalize what he was doing and ignore the fact that *someone* was opening that door behind him. Keeping her gaze on him was damn near impossible when all she wanted to do was look away.

As he reached the elastic band of her work pants, he lifted them a fraction with his hand. Then he grasped a section and slid his knife into it. He didn't stop until he'd reached the hem by her ankle. He stared off into space as he spoke. "Abigail was...personal. After I finished with her, I left the country for a while. Work."

"What do you do?" She inwardly cursed herself for interrupting him when his gaze snapped back to hers, full of anger. That's when she saw Grant step into the room, gun in hand.

Her captor's back was to the door, all his focus solely on her. He smiled, reminding her of a shark. "I'm a plastic surgeon. Occasionally I do follow up work at *your* hospital." His voice was mildly taunting.

That shocked her, but she didn't let her surprise show. She kept her face blank as Grant raised his gun, pointing it directly at the man's head.

"Drop the knife or I put a bullet in your head," Grant ordered softly, his voice a razor sharp edge that left no doubt he'd do exactly that.

The man froze, still holding the knife. Surprise and rage registered on his face as he stared at Belle. His expression immediately turned cold, calculating. "How did you find me?" he asked, his eyes never wavering from Belle's and the knife hand never moving.

"You're not as smart as you think. Drop. The. Knife." Grant took a silent step toward the guy, his weapon firmly in his hands.

"I won't go to jail." He moved lightning fast, lunging at her as he raised the knife to plunge into her chest.

On instinct Belle closed her eyes and turned her face away, tensing for the cutting pain. Three loud bangs reverberated around the room. As something heavy fell on her she opened her eyes and let out a brief scream.

She heard Grant curse but could only stare at the man draped across her bare stomach. His body was heavy and unmoving. She sucked in a breath and wiggled, trying to somehow move the monster off her. Blood dripped all over her as Grant shoved the body off her and onto the floor.

"Are you okay?"

"Get me out of the restraints!" Untamed panic welled inside her. It was like a living, breathing thing ready to completely take over. She tried to tell herself to stop struggling, that she was safe now, but she was about to have a serious breakdown if he didn't get her free.

As he bent down over the body she could see him searching the man's pockets until finally he popped up with a small silver key grasped tightly in his hand. It felt like an eternity passed until he'd completely freed her wrists and ankles. Unable to stop the cry that rose in her throat she attempted to sit up but Grant caught her underneath her back and pulled her close to his chest in an almost crushing hug. He murmured soothing words as he stroked her back and lifted her up.

Sobs wracked her body and the more she tried to get herself under control the worse it was. She was vaguely aware of him carrying her outside. When the sun nearly blinded her, she blinked, her tears drying from the shock and pulled back from her death grip around his neck.

"Are you... Did he hurt you?" Grant's voice cracked on the last word, his eyes filled with agony.

She shook her head, fighting to breathe, to get a grip. "No. Thanks to you," she whispered, looking around at her surroundings.

Grant had just walked them out of a simple looking shed into a giant backyard filled with lush greenery, overgrown rosebushes and other foliage. The back of the house was a Queen Anne style home. Everything looked so...*normal*. There were no noises from the neighbors, the sun was shining and she could hear a dog barking nearby. Despite the warmth from being outside, she shivered uncontrollably.

Grant sat on a patio chair and cradled her in his arms. She'd stopped crying but couldn't seem to let go of him. All she could concentrate on was the feel of his strong arms keeping her in a warm, tight embrace, the beat of his heartbeat and his familiar scent. She knew they should do something like call the police, but she felt safe and secure and refused to let go of that. Just his being there grounded her and counteracted the raw panic threatening to burst through her. In her head she knew she was safe, but her body was having a hard time catching up.

The sound of footsteps and then a surprised curse made her jerk her head up. Carlito rounded the corner of the house, gun in hand. He looked at them cautiously but Grant must have motioned with his head because he nodded and continued back to the shed.

Once he was out of sight two more men crept around the corner of the house, both carrying guns. She stared at them, briefly wondering why they looked so familiar when she realized she'd seen them in the pictures at Grant's house. These were his brothers. And she was almost completely exposed and covered in blood.

The way Grant held her gave her a little cover, but she couldn't bear for strangers to see her like this. Bury-

ing her face in Grant's neck, she tried to hold back another sob.

There was a rustling behind her and Grant murmured something she couldn't understand, but when he
started to pull back she instinctively fought to stay closer
to him.

"Honey, I've got a shirt for you. I want you to put it
on." His voice was quiet next to her ear.

"Okay," she rasped out, grateful she'd found her
voice. After slipping on a big collared black shirt with a
Red Stone logo on it she finally looked around again.
Both his brothers had their backs to her as they stood at
alert. The tallest one was missing a shirt and it slowly
registered that he'd given it to her.

Before she could say thank you, Grant's former partner was stalking back across the yard on his radio. Then
all the men started talking at once. Grant still held her
tight, but he was just as involved in the conversation as
everyone else.

They asked her a few questions and she must have
answered because she received nods. Eventually paramedics and a whole lot of uniformed officers showed up.
People kept asking her questions and she continued answering when all she wanted to do was curl into a ball
and hide. When they practically forced her into an ambulance, Grant never left her side. He rode with her all
the way to the hospital and was quite insistent that he'd

be staying in her room. She hadn't been injured—well she was emotionally fried—but they wanted to keep her overnight anyway and run a toxicology report to see what her kidnapper had given her. She probably could have fought them but she didn't have the energy.

A doctor she knew eventually gave her a couple pills he said would help her sleep and she didn't even question. She hated taking drugs but right now she felt as if she might implode if she didn't shut the outside world out for a few hours. Sleep was the only way to do that. Eventually she drifted off, secure because Grant was next to her bedside. His face was a mask of worry and she wanted to tell him she was fine, but she simply didn't have the strength.

* * *

Grant shot Belle another glance as he steered into his driveway. She'd been thoroughly checked out at the hospital and finally released around noon. While she was physically fine she'd been incredibly quiet. Not that he blamed her, it just killed him seeing her so subdued and unlike herself. If he could, he'd kill that psycho Matthew Brown all over again. A common name for a man who by all accounts had looked and acted normal.

From what Carlito had told him, the plastic surgeon had been living in South America the last few years—

which was why there was such a huge span of time in between the first two victims. Unfortunately it seemed they technically weren't the first two victims. From the brief research Carlito had done it looked like Brown had killed women all across Brazil, Chile, Peru and Bolivia over the last five years. His MO was the same for a lot of unsolved murders in all those countries. There were probably many that weren't even reported but once this story went international Grant had a feeling they'd discover even more killings.

That wasn't something he wanted to think about though. Belle was alive and safe and a monster was dead. He'd gone down to the police station last night while Belle had been sleeping—only once his brother Porter had arrived to stay with her—to make an official statement. He should have had to go right after the shooting but Carlito and his former boss had pulled a lot of strings to let him ride to the hospital with Belle. Of course it didn't hurt that his father had a lot of contacts with the Miami PD too.

His entire family wanted to meet her and she needed to call her own family soon. He'd tried to broach the subject but she'd refused. She'd said she just wanted a day of rest and sleep before they all rushed over. Considering everything she'd been through in the past week and how well she was holding up, he figured it was her business how she handled things with her family. But he knew from experience that the longer she put it off the worse their reactions would be.

"I need to get some clothes," she murmured, the sound of her voice surprising him.

He didn't stop until they were in his driveway. "I hope it's okay, but...I had my sister-in-law get a bag of stuff for you. I used the keys you'd left behind. I wasn't sure how late they'd discharge you so I had her grab some clothes. She'd planned to bring it up to the hospital but when the doctor let you go she just left it at my place."

She blinked at him, her expression one of surprise. Crap, maybe he'd really overstepped his bounds. "Sorry."

A slight smile played across her lips, drawing his attention to them. "No, it's really sweet. Thank you. So you don't mind me staying at your place?"

He snorted and got out of the vehicle. If she hadn't been staying here, he'd be at her place whether in her bed or camped out in her living room. After the hell she'd been through, he was going to be her shadow for the foreseeable future. He still couldn't get the image of that psycho with the knife poised above her body or her strapped down and helpless. Rubbing his eyes as if it would somehow help, he mentally shook himself. Before he'd made it around to her side she'd shut her door and was rounding the front of his vehicle.

Nervous to touch her too much, he kept a little distance and opened the door that led into his kitchen. She gave him a curious look as she passed by him, but didn't reach out to touch him either. He was so nervous around her, unsure if he should make any sort of physical gesture toward her. The need to gather her in his arms and comfort her was so strong, but his gut told him it would be a mistake. She'd been so closed off since she'd woken up this morning and he felt lost. Not that anyone could blame her for being withdrawn. He just didn't want to screw up their relationship because he'd misjudged her needs.

Wrapping her arms around herself and looking adorable in the one-size-too-big scrubs the hospital had given her, Belle leaned against the center island and watched him.

"You hungry?"

"Not for food," she said quietly, a spark of something dangerous in her eyes.

"Ah..." Unsure what to do with his hands, he opened the refrigerator and stared blindly inside. He wondered if he'd misunderstood her. "We've got—"

A soft hand settled on his non-scarred arm. Her fingers slightly dug into his skin. "Grant. I want you to touch me, to make love to me. Right now."

Shutting the door he turned to face her and he couldn't help the worry that slithered through him. "You should be resting, Belle. I know you said he didn't...assault you, but you're not thinking clearly."

Her eyebrows rose for a fraction of a second before she glared at him. "Don't you dare tell me what I'm thinking or what I need. I know exactly what I want right now and it's *you*. That monster could have done a hell of a lot worse to me and yeah, I'm still pretty shaken up by everything, but I need to feel you inside me. I want you to wipe away everything that happened."

Grant swallowed hard, knowing he couldn't deny her anything. Even if he feared that he might be pushing her too far too fast. She'd just had a week from hell, she should be up in bed recovering, but when she slid her arms up his chest and wrapped them around his neck he knew he was lost.

They might be going to bed but she wouldn't be resting or sleeping. He tried to be gentle but when she wrapped her legs around his waist he only stumbled a few steps until they ran into the island. She sat on the edge of the granite countertop so he released his grip from her hips.

Belle tore at his shirt almost in a frenzy, her hands trembling. Something twisted inside his chest as he stilled her hands. "Let me take care of you."

"I—" He put a finger to her lips before lifting his shirt off. He might still cringe a little at the thought of baring himself to her, especially with sunlight streaming in through the kitchen blinds, but her gaze was heated and needy, alleviating any worries.

Grasping the hem of her top, he slowly lifted it off. She raised her arms, letting him pull it completely free. She wasn't wearing a bra underneath, something he'd known, but seeing her gorgeous breasts still made him suck in a breath. He could be gentle but they definitely weren't making it to the bedroom this first time.

He leaned down and sucked one of her already hard nipples in between his teeth. She drew in a ragged breath as she arched her back, pushing herself farther into his mouth. Cupping her other breast with his hand, he slowly strummed her nipple with his thumb.

His entire body tensed with the need to take her hard and fast but that wasn't what she needed right now. Even if she thought she did. Flicking his tongue over her sensitive skin, he circled her areola but stopped stroking her actual nipple. He did the same with her other breast, just teased her everywhere else.

Belle finally let out a growl of frustration as she tightened her legs around his waist. She tugged him tight against her, grinding against his erection. "I think you get off on teasing me," she groaned.

He smiled against her breast before kissing a path down her long scar. She shuddered each time his lips brushed over her skin. Without looking up at her, he pressed on her shoulder, easing her back. "Lay down," he ordered, not leaving any room for argument.

As she stretched out on the island top, he reached the top of her pants. Using his teeth and hands, he grasped the elastic material and tugged the pants down her legs. When she tried to squeeze her legs together, he grinned. "Oh no, I get to see all of you."

He took her ankles and guided her feet up to the edge of the counter so that her thighs were splayed open and her glistening pussy was on display for him. Looking up at her face, he saw a trace of unease there. Not directed at him, he was sure, but whatever was going on in her head, he needed to calm her worries. He knew exactly how to distract her.

Unable to wait any longer he bent down and didn't bother with easing her into anything. He immediately focused on her clit, teasing and licking without any mercy. The little bud was swollen with arousal and peeking out from behind her slick lips and the moment his tongue touched it, she jerked against his face.

Tasting her like this was heaven. Hell, just being near her was. When he thought he might have lost her, he'd known he loved her. It was probably too soon and he'd never been in love before but he knew what he felt. The all-consuming and overpowering need to be with her, to protect her was damn scary. He had a feeling he'd never completely stop worrying about her safety, but he could live with anything if it meant she was in his life.

With each stroke of his tongue, her back arched off the counter and her thighs squeezed against him. Her body was shaking and he'd barely gotten started. When she grabbed onto his head, he smiled against her wetness and slowly eased a finger inside her.

Her fingers tightened in his hair and her breathing became more erratic. She was so tight around just his finger when he imagined sliding his cock into her, he couldn't fight his own shudder. God, he needed inside her soon. But first he wanted her to climax.

With the steady rhythm he'd learned she loved, he moved his finger in and out of her. When she started moaning his name and slammed her palms down on the counter, he smiled against her clit, still not easing up on his pressure. She was close.

As her inner walls started clenching tighter around him, he lightly pressed his teeth against her little bundle of nerves. That did it. She completely pushed off the counter as her cream rushed over his finger. Her climax was sharp and intense, her inner muscles spasming out of control.

Sitting up, she grasped his shoulders and tugged him to her mouth. Hungrily, he kissed her as she grappled with his belt and pants. Helping her, he shoved at them, but he'd barely gotten them down his legs before she grasped his waist.

Her fingers dug into him as she pulled him to her. As his cock pushed deep inside her wet heat, he stilled, enjoying the feel of her clenching around him. Burying his head against her neck, he inhaled her sweet scent. That raspberries and vanilla scent was subtle now, but it wrapped around him with a soothing purity.

"I love you," he whispered, unable to look at her face as he said it.

Belle sucked in a deep breath so before she could respond he pulled his head back then crushed his mouth over hers. He didn't want to hear her response if she didn't feel the same and there was no way in hell he was pulling out of her.

Feeling a little out of control he thrust into her over and over as their mouths tangled with each other. He felt frantic as he slammed into her, but was unable to control his need and hunger. With her, he lost all sense of restraint.

When she dug her fingers into his ass, raking her fingernails along his skin, he came. His orgasm was as uncontrolled as hers had been. With her name on his lips he emptied himself inside her in long, hot strokes. Even when he'd spent everything he had in her, his hips still blindly rocked against her until she wrapped her arms tight around him, pulling him impossibly close.

"I love you, too, in case you're wondering," she said, slightly giggling. When she did, her inner walls tightened on his half-hard cock, making him shudder.

He pulled his head back so he could fully look at her. The love and trust he saw took his breath away. After shoving off the rest of his clothes he lifted her off the counter and headed for the stairs. He might need a short break but he didn't plan on leaving his bed for a long time.

CHAPTER TEN

Balancing three beers in her hands, Belle nudged open the door that led to Grant's backyard. His patio was packed with his brothers, their significant others, his father and of course her own giant family. She couldn't even attempt to count how many of her relatives were there. There were so many cousins, aunts and uncles—but no members of the Balis family which would have been odd under other circumstances but her mother was still enraged at Paulos for trying to manhandle her. Considering everything else that had happened in the last couple weeks—that was just a blip on her radar now.

Her family was so loud she wanted to be a little embarrassed but she couldn't muster up anything. She loved all of them. And Grant didn't care and that was all that mattered. Weaving through the laughing, talking people she made her way to Grant who was by his massive grill—where her father and brothers all hovered, staring at it with envy. She handed a beer to Grant and her father and kept the last for herself.

"Hey, where's mine?" Alek, one of her brother's grumbled. At twenty-nine he was the youngest of her three brothers but still five years older than her.

She smiled sweetly. "Your legs aren't broken."

Her father snorted in agreement. "What's the matter with you? Your sister shouldn't be doing anything. Get your own drink and grab her a chair while you're at it." Then he looked at her admonishingly as Alek hurried away. "You shouldn't be doing anything, least of all getting me a drink. I thought you were by the pool resting."

Odell and Dennis, her other brothers, both nodded in agreement. "I'll grab you a lounge chair," Odell murmured, hurrying off.

She contemplated protesting but knew it would be futile. She was used to their over protectiveness.

Grant shot her a sideways glance and she could tell he was fighting a smile. But he wisely didn't tell her she needed to rest. While she might not have gone back to work yet—the hospital had forced her to take two weeks off with full pay—she wasn't an invalid and she needed to keep moving. If she didn't, her mother and aunts would descend on her wanting to know when Grant would be proposing.

Belle snorted to herself. Her mother had certainly gotten over her demand that Belle marry someone Greek once she met Grant. He'd actually surprised her with his ability to charm her formidable mother. Of course it probably had more to do with the fact that he'd saved Belle's life from a serial killer. Her mother had been cooking like a madwoman the past two weeks. A covered dish for Belle and one for Grant every single day. As if either of them could eat that much. And Grant didn't just tolerate her family; he seemed to genuinely adore them, which was icing on the cake.

Shaking her head, Belle kissed her father on the cheek then hurried away, blending into the crowd. It was amazing so many people fit in Grant's backyard, but a few of her cousins had taken up residence in the pool and definitely weren't leaving anytime soon. Those same cousins were flirting mercilessly with Vincent and Travis. Vincent was eating it up but Travis looked uncomfortable and a little scared. A six foot plus giant of a man with too many tattoos and piercings to count should not be intimidated by her petite cousins. She might have felt sorry for him, but her cousins were all gorgeous and there were worse ways to be tortured.

After stopping to talk to half a dozen people, she found herself in the kitchen again grabbing two more bottles of wine. As she set them on the counter she eyed the contents of the fridge, debating if she should bring out another platter of the cheese eggplant rolls her mom had brought. Grant would be done grilling soon but she didn't think it was possible to have too much food tonight. Not with this crowd. Grabbing it, she started to nudge the door shut when large hands closed on her waist from behind.

Instinctively she jumped then recognized that masculine, very familiar spicy scent of Grant. Grinning, she leaned back into him. "Why aren't you manning the grill?"

"Our dads have taken over. I decided to let them fight for it so I could find you," he murmured close to her ear, the heat of his breath dancing across her skin. "I've barely seen you all day." He almost sounded pouty, which she found incredibly adorable.

Setting the platter down on the closest counter, she turned and wrapped her arms around him, linking her fingers behind his neck. "I've got to be the hostess while you're cooking."

"You *should* be sitting somewhere with your feet up," he murmured, but there wasn't much heat in his voice.

"Hush. You know I'm fine." They'd had enough sex the past couple weeks that she knew he wasn't worried about her being physically fragile.

His grip on her waist tightened as he pulled her flush against his body and bent to feather kisses along her jaw. "I wonder if anyone would miss us for about half an hour."

She chuckled, her own hold on him increasing. "Ah, the *real* reason you were looking for me."

He gently tugged one of her earlobes between his teeth but froze at the sound of the door opening and slamming. Belle leaned back to find her mom fighting a grin. Eirene Manikas was simply an older version of Belle and had the intimidating look down to an art, though she wasn't using it now. She just clicked her tongue at them and picked up the wine bottles. "If I were you, Grant, I'd hurry back to that grill. I think my husband might be doing some permanent damage."

Fighting her own smile, Belle took Grant's hand in hers and tugged him outside, ignoring his groan of displeasure. The man was insatiable and in a few hours they'd have the house back to themselves and plenty of uninterrupted bedroom time. For now, she was enjoying being with her family and the man she loved.

And she was desperately trying to pretend she hadn't accidentally seen the two-carat princess cut, flawless diamond engagement ring she'd found in one of Grant's drawers days ago—that he was currently carrying around. She'd felt it earlier and realized what it was.

A few times that morning he'd acted all nervous and patted his pants leg as if he was afraid he'd lost it. She couldn't even imagine when he'd had time to buy it, but she was glad they were on the same page. She certainly hadn't expected him to buy a ring this soon, but it didn't surprise her. When Grant decided on something, that was that.

Most people would say it was too soon, but she knew she loved him more than anything. When he finally worked up the courage to ask her to marry him, her answer would be a definite yes. She'd already basically moved in to his place. Eventually she'd worry about renting out her house or even selling it, or maybe they'd move into hers and sell his—but all that stuff was just extraneous crap she couldn't even focus on at the moment. Considering she'd survived being stalked then almost tortured and killed by a serial killer—everything else was completely manageable. Well, as long as Grant was in her life.

COMPLETE BOOKLIST

Red Stone Security Series
No One to Trust
Danger Next Door
Fatal Deception
Miami, Mistletoe & Murder
His to Protect
Breaking Her Rules
Protecting His Witness
Sinful Seduction
Under His Protection
Deadly Fallout
Sworn to Protect

The Serafina: Sin City Series
First Surrender
Sensual Surrender
Sweetest Surrender
Dangerous Surrender

Deadly Ops Series
Targeted
Bound to Danger
Chasing Danger (novella)
Shattered Duty
Edge of Danger

A Covert Affair

Non-series Romantic Suspense
Running From the Past
Dangerous Secrets
Killer Secrets
Deadly Obsession
Danger in Paradise
His Secret Past
Retribution

Paranormal Romance
Destined Mate
Protector's Mate
A Jaguar's Kiss
Tempting the Jaguar
Enemy Mine
Heart of the Jaguar

Moon Shifter Series
Alpha Instinct
Lover's Instinct (novella)
Primal Possession
Mating Instinct
His Untamed Desire (novella)
Avenger's Heat
Hunter Reborn
Protective Instinct (novella)

Darkness Series
Darkness Awakened

Taste of Darkness
Beyond the Darkness
Hunted by Darkness
Into the Darkness

ABOUT THE AUTHOR

Katie Reus is the *New York Times* and *USA Today* bestselling author of the Red Stone Security series, the Moon Shifter series and the Deadly Ops series. She fell in love with romance at a young age thanks to books she pilfered from her mom's stash. Years later she loves reading romance almost as much as she loves writing it.

However, she didn't always know she wanted to be a writer. After changing majors many times, she finally graduated summa cum laude with a degree in psychology. Not long after that she discovered a new love. Writing. She now spends her days writing dark paranormal romance and sexy romantic suspense. For more information on Katie please visit her website: www.katiereus.com. Also find her on twitter @katiereus or visit her on facebook at: www.facebook.com/katiereusauthor.

Made in the USA
Middletown, DE
15 June 2023

32655105R00104